Shadow Blade: LitRPG Adventure Fantasy

LitRPG: Shadow For Hire, Volume 4

Adam Drake

Published by Adam Drake, 2018.

This is a work of fiction. Similarities to real people, places, or events are entirely coincidental.

SHADOW BLADE: LITRPG ADVENTURE FANTASY

First edition. August 21, 2018.

Copyright © 2018 Adam Drake.

ISBN: 979-8201175214

Written by Adam Drake.

Shadow Blade
Shadow For Hire Book 4
by
Adam Drake
Copyright 2018 © Adam Drake

Shadow Blade

Shadow For Hire Series

A hallowed weapon hidden in a jungle hell.

Forced to prove my worthiness to an elite group of players, I must earn the right to enter one of the most notorious locations in the game.

The Emerald Caldera has a fearsome reputation for chewing up would-be adventurers and quickly sending them back to the newbie zone. Filled with dungeon temples, monstrous beasts and dark-magic cults, the jungles of this mysterious island are deserving of respect.

And I must plunge headlong into them because it is here where I can find the next elusive item in my Legendary Armor Set:

The Shadow Blade

CHAPTER ONE

I logged into the game to find myself on the edge of Hell.

Before me was a vast ocean of molten lava which steamed and hissed. Its surface writhed like a living thing. The air above wavered from the intense heat and the smell of sulfur was strong enough for me to readjust the olfactory preferences on my simulation suit.

I crouched on solid ground of cracked, weathered stone. The lava lapped at its edge, only a few paces from me. At my back was a large angular boulder, and to both sides the stone shore curved behind out of sight.

Taking in these bleak surroundings, I sighed with relief. My avatar was in the exact spot I'd left her when I logged off to sleep six hours earlier.

Since I wasn't in a safezone, logging out here meant my avatar remained in the game for five full minutes, helpless and at the mercy of any passing threat. Fortunately, I'd chosen a good hiding spot, although I barely slept, wondering if I'd made a mistake.

Wanting to make a quick assessment of my situation, I activated my Shadow ability, and slowly stood to peer around the boulder.

I was on one side of a large stone platform in the middle of the lava, near featureless save for several boulders studding its perimeter. Opposite to me towered a pair of large wide iron doors set into an outcropping of rock. The outcropping extended away from the platform like a handle on a frying pan, its upper reaches vanishing into the dark sulfuric clouds which hung low above.

Being completely surrounded by the molten lake there was no other way off the platform except through those doors. They were closed and securely locked. And I didn't possess the means to open them.

I was trapped.

Laughing with delight I nearly clapped my hands together which would've broken my Shadow. Nothing had changed in the last six hours since I logged out. The doors hadn't been opened which meant my quarry was still on their way. My timing couldn't have been better.

My mind at ease I crouched again, resting my back against the boulder. I was in the Dungeon of Xorrox, a ridiculously massive network of caves and tunnels meant to test the most hardy of adventurers. It was filled with demons, rock golems and even the occasional fire drake.

At the very bottom of the dungeon was this platform, its end point, and the gateway to the final dungeon boss encounter who waited behind those doors. Xorrox.

My being here was suicidal, I knew that. At level 46 I fell way short of the recommended minimum of 55 for entering. It was also a group setting because of its difficulty. As many as thirty or so players were needed to fight its many dangers with the hope that enough would survive to get to this very platform.

And yet here I was, a low level Shadow standing at the end of a truly nasty group dungeon. It hadn't been easy, not at all. Any one of the creatures in here could one-shot me and I'd find myself back at the newbie zone, right quick.

I managed it by staying in Shadow form and inching my way through its complex of caves, from the entrance all the way to this desolate stone platform. The entire endeavor took three full days.

There were many times I almost got caught and died on the spot. Fire drakes have a nasty habit of randomly scorching nearby walls just for the fun of it. Walls and shadows are my main security and stumbling upon a fire drake with a penchant for burping up death at the walls of its lair was terrifying.

Yet, I made it. There'd been several hundred creatures I snuck by. As a result, my Sneak skill spiked, being around so many higher level threats. When I started it sat at Level 7, with 42% progression. Now it was Level 8, with 12% progression. An amazing rise considering how difficult it is to increase a skill at such high a level.

But why risk it at all? What could be the point of wilfully risking permadeath delving into a place that was way out of my league?

I'd like to say I was on a job, hired to get here which I was. But the real reason is more telling than that.

A small flashing indicator dinged loudly at the corner of my vision, making me jump. Someone was requesting an audio chat. I'd originally muted my entire communications within the game so not to get distracting dancing around death. But there was only one person who was allowed to do so. My client.

"Hello, Shwenn," I said, opening the channel. "Can't sleep?"

"Are they there yet?" A woman's voice asked by way of greeting. She sounded agitated and high strung.

"No, not yet. But I wouldn't worry. They'll come," I said.

"How can you be sure?" Shwenn said. "Maybe they wiped on the way down. That place is dangerous, you know."

I wanted to point out the obvious that I knew first hand the dungeon was dangerous, but didn't feel like getting into it with her. "I'm sure they haven't wiped because I just checked their guild tracker. Most of them are still alive, amazingly, and should arrive soon." I hoped they did, or I was out in a big way.

"Right, I didn't think of that," Shwenn said. "It's just that I really need this to work, you know? The guys are counting on it."

"Counting on me, you mean?"

"Yeah, counting on you. You've got to pull this off, there might never be another opportunity, again."

"I'm aware, Shwenn. I'll do my best."

"But how can I be sure?"

"Because I'm talking to you, aren't I? Look, when these clowns show up we're good to go. No problem. I've got this handled." Besides, it wasn't like there was anyone else down in this hellhole to do the job.

"Right, sorry," she said, laughing nervously. "I'm glad you're there. We're all glad you're there." Then, as if she realized the danger I'd put myself in she asked, "So, how did it go?"

"The relic?"

"Yeah."

"It went fine. No one saw me come in." The entrance to the Dungeon was guarded by a large group of high level players whose sole purpose was to extort groups trying to get in. Their demands were high to the point of being unrealistic. But the rewards for finishing the dungeon canceled that out, and many groups paid.

For me, I spent four hours tiptoeing past the guards and then through the magical barricade which they'd cast over the entrance. I had Shwenn to thank for that. She'd given my a relic of Bend Magic before I'd started, an expensive item. Pressing the relic against the barrier formed a small hole to appear which I crawled through. When the relic crumbled after its use, I knew there would be no turning back.

"That's good. That's great," Shwenn said. "So you're on the platform now?"

"Of course."

"How in the heck did you get there?" her tone was one of awe, as it should be.

The platform was located in the center of a vast chamber, its walls so far apart I couldn't even see them from where I crouched. There's only one known way to reach it, and that can only be activated by a group with at least twenty four members present, the minimum needed to gain entry to Xorrox's den.

There was no way I could do that, being a solo Shadow, and all. But through my research of the dungeon I discovered several natural stone bridges, or beams, that crisscrossed its upper reaches.

To get to them, I climbed up from one of several small tunnel openings that dotted the chamber's colossal walls. Using a pair of daggers and my Sure Foot ability, I pulled myself up, grumbling and cursing the whole way. This bumped my Climbing skill to Level 7, with 22% progression. Once at the right stone beam I eased across until I was directly above the platform.

Then I jumped. Crazy, sure. But using my Freefall ability to slow my descent, and a well timed Health Boost which doubled my hit points, I landed safely. Kind of. More like a splat. The impact shattered my avatar's legs and broke her spine along with other bones and internal organs. I'd gone from 1,250 hit points to 22. Close. Another few feet of height and I'd be rerolling my character.

Using a large stash of healing potions I'd brought just for the occasion, I nursed my avatar back to health over several hours. But I'd made it. I was on the platform.

Instead of explaining all of this to Shwenn, who I knew was only asking out of politeness, I said, "I almost died. But I figured our deal was worth the risk."

"Yes!" Shwenn said. "Our deal is solid, don't you worry."

The fact she said I shouldn't worry made me worry. The deal was why I went through this entire escapade to begin with. The deal was everything. "I trust you, Shwenn. You've got one of the highest Honor ratings I've seen. And the end result is to both our benefit."

Suddenly, I noticed a large sloping object appear above the surface of the lava ahead, then vanish. Alarm bells rang off in my head. Was there something actually in that stuff?

"I'm glad you feel that way," she said. "Deal breaking is not my thing, as my record shows. But, really, how did you-." She suddenly went quiet, then said, "They're there! It just popped up on their tracker! They're coming to you now!"

Keeping one eye on the spot the thing had appeared at, I stood slowly to check the platform. At first I didn't see anything. Then, off in the sulfuric haze, I saw movement. A large slab of rock bobbed out of the lava. Then another. The two slabs merged together, followed by third. A land bridge was forming across the molten lake from some distant point, and it was slowly coming this way.

The group crossing.

"You're right," I said, feeling excited. "I gotta go now, Shwenn. We'll meet at Crow's Fall as we discussed."

"Oh, okay! Just remember, you have to pull this off or-."

I cut the channel. Hearing how I couldn't screw things up would just make me overthink the situation.

From the unseen end of the rock bridge, people emerged, following it along. The first sign of their presence was the light cast from spells, probably mass heals and protective auras to keep the group from succumbing to the incredible heat.

Then I saw them in more detail as they cautiously made their way toward the platform.

They made it. Admittedly I had a niggling doubt these chuckleheads might die along the way, but I felt a sense of elation seeing them approach. Now I could move on to the next phase of my plan.

Movement at the corner of my eye made me tear my focus from the group to look.

A long orange hump appeared in the lava a dozen or so paces from me. Transfixed, I watched in horror as two black eyes opened on it. They were looking at me.

I gasped in surprise. What the hell was that thing? I checked myself over and confirmed my Shadow form was still very much on. The little eye-icon at the side of my vision was faded, indicating my Shadow was fully active. Technically, I was invisible, and provided I didn't move around much, it would stay that way.

But the strange thing in the lava seemed to be staring right at me.

The hairs on the back of my neck prickled within my simulation suit. This wasn't good.

The growing land-bridge finally reached the platform and merged to its edge. A cavalcade of players marched over it and onto shore. They looked beat up, for the most part, but happy. The odds had been against them even getting to this place.

Players, mounts and pets spread out onto the platform, all looking for a spot to rest. Potions were quaffed and more healing spells cast.

With the inane name of 'Try And Catch Us', this guild had been on my radar for several days. They'd been making a scene on the forums and news-feeds that an attempt on the Dungeon of Xorrox would be made, and that the big boss was going down. Doing some digging I was happy to find the majority of their players were quite competent when it came to clearing big dungeons. The fact they were on the platform was proof.

One of the treasures Xorrox drops is a small statue of a coiled snake, a coveted object. It's part of a set of two which is required to unlock a very special instance in the game. The Emerald Caldera.

Access to the Emerald Caldera is highly sought after, since it's rumored to be not just challenging, but very rewarding in loot. Yet, it can only be entered once per year by a group of no more than six players. Getting into such a group with access to the Caldera is nearly impossible.

Shwenn already owned the first statue and needed the second one. Most guilds like Try And Catch Us would never sell or trade such an object if they had it. They'd use it themselves.

So when I saw Shwenn's posting on the Trade forums desperate to obtain the second statue I told here I'd get it for her. But what I wanted in trade was a spot in her group to the Caldera.

She agreed, and I immediately looked for a guild who were raiding the Dungeon of Xorrox and found Try And Catch Us. I knew that if I could somehow get into position when they opened Xorrox's doors, I'd have a shot at sneaking in.

Which led to my suicidal dungeon crawl to get to the platform. So far so good.

But all of that was in the immediate past. What concerned me know was the immediate future. Particularly the strange creature eyeing me from the lava. It hadn't moved or even blinked. To be honest, I couldn't tell if it could actually see me and just happened to be looking in my exact direction.

But I don't believe in coincidences.

Behind me I heard the Try And Catch Us leader shout for everyone to get ready. They were going in.

But I was too focused on the beast in the lava which suddenly started to swim straight at me. I looked around for a place to run, but there was only the open space around the boulder. The other players were of a higher level than me. Which meant they had a better chance of seeing me moving about, even in full Shadow form.

But I couldn't stay in that spot any longer.

As the creature reached the shore, I ran off to the right, cursing under my breath. The thing surged out of the lava, bringing a wave of the molten liquid with it. It looked like a giant gecko, but made of heated stone.

I sprinted around the rear of the assembled group who's entire focus was on the door and their leader. As the monster crashed onto the platform they all turned to look in surprise.

I prayed none of them looked directly at me and that I'd made enough distance to go unnoticed, but I couldn't be sure.

"Trash mob!" somebody shouted.

"Let's clean house!" Shouted another.

The large group immediately engaged with the creature as I fled toward another boulder. As I scurried around it, my apprehension was through the roof. Had I been seen?

I heard the noise of fighting and the roar of the gecko beast. In less than a minute, there was a tremendous crash, and the ground shook, followed by cheers.

Carefully, I peeked around the boulder to find players looting the creature's corpse.

"Sucks!" Someone said. "Not worth the effort."

The group then returned to their positions on the platform and my wary eyes scanned over them. No one had seen me!

Their leader, a Holy Knight who paradoxically was geared in a full ebony suit of armor took out a bright red gem and set it into a small nook in one of the doors.

The great doors slowly rumbled open, and the group cheered again. Cautiously, they entered.

I'd moved to a boulder closest to the door and crouched there, waiting. After the last player entered, the doors slowly began to swing shut.

Bolting from my hiding spot I ran for the shrinking opening. I had to wait as long as I could before entering in case someone was watching.

Just as the doors were closing I dived through the small space and landed in a roll. I quickly moved to a dark corner and crouched.

Behind me, the huge doors clicked shut.

I looked around, half expecting to be caught. But the group had already moved on past a bend in the entryway tunnel, their shadows playing along the walls. They hadn't even bothered to post a rear guard to watch.

I love cocky guilds, I thought to myself.

Then, keeping to the shadows, I followed.

CHAPTER TWO

The cavernous tunnel extended ahead. The group marched on headless of their flank or even bothering to search for secret doors. Their focus was entirely on getting to Xorrox.

My research showed there were three minor bosses to face before the big guy, and as the guild turned a corner, I could hear them launch into battle with the first.

Carefully, I approached the sound of spells and clashing of steel which filled the air. I hurried ahead to catch the fight, but even before I peeked around the corner it was all over.

A large three-armed titan was splayed out on the ground. Around him, players picked through the loot items it'd dropped while others held their noses up and continued on.

As the last player left, I slinked over to the corpse and checked it for any leftovers. Other than the sub-silver piece trash, there was one small sword left behind.

You have acquired an item: Short Sword of Defense
Required Strength: 25
Damage 40-65
+15% Parry
Value: 3 Gold Pieces.

I shrugged and stuffed it in my pack. That makes for 3 gold pieces I didn't have before.

Again, the sounds of combat echoed off the walls. I hustled down the tunnel to find the group finishing off a stone lion which crumbled into large pieces when it died.

Once the group left, I looked through the large rocks of the lion corpse and found three small potions and a pair of clawed knuckles, carved from stone.

You have acquired an item: Small Health Shot Potion(x3)
Heals 50 hit points instantly. Cannot be stacked.

The third and final minor boss proved to be a bit more of a challenge. A towering humanoid-shaped demon, wielding a large twin-bladed axe, kept the group on their toes. Once they realized this wasn't going to be a pushover, the players got their act together and organized a better attack.

The demon, for its part, had several nasty tricks up its demonic sleeve. The twisted horns on its head would occasional fire an arc of lighting at the players near the back, which was composed mostly of ranged attackers and spell casters. Several of them took serious damage while a cleric was rendered unconscious.

The twin-bladed axe also would suddenly become a whirling buzzsaw that the demon would thrust down at the warriors hacking at its knees.

Still, this was a tough group, and they hadn't come all this way, and through so much, to wipe on a minor boss. In short order they wore the demon down until they killed it. The final death blow was given by an anthropomorphic eagle Slayer, who used a glowing blue broadsword to cleave the demon's head in two.

The loot this time garnered more attention and debate, particularly over the huge axe. Eventually, a centaur Barbarian won that prize after a quick game of determination dice. The other players picked through the rest then continued on.

On inspection I found the corpse of the demon picked clean. But as I turned to follow the others my vision snagged on the horns on the creature's head. They were short, about an arm's span in length, and the dark material they were made of was marbled with deep blue veins.

On impulse I grabbed at one and pulled. It came out of the demon's head with a pop, and I admired my luck.

You have acquired and item: Demon Horn of Lightning
Required Intelligence: 25
Durability 40/40
Casts Lightening Bolt – Cooldown 45 seconds.
Damage: 85-120
Value: 85 Gold Pieces

I whistled in amazement. This was sweet. Unfortunately for me, my Intelligence was only 15 and too low to use it. Still, it was worth a good chunk of gold.

The other horn popped out as well. Chuckling, I put both the horns in my pack. "Arrogant guilds," I said, shaking my head. I needed to stalk these clowns more often.

As I entered the tunnel, I found it empty up ahead. Suppressing a mild panic attack I sprinted forward until reaching a wide curve. Carefully tip-toeing around it, I was surprised to find the entire group loitering in a large chamber just outside a massive square doorway.

It took me a second for my brain to catch up. They were taking a rest break before the final showdown. Some players would step out of their simulation suits without logging off and go do their business. While this happened, the group would chat amongst themselves and cast last minute auras and spells.

Happy I hadn't lost them, I squatted down in a shadowy corner a short distance away. Here, I was totally invisible and confident that even if they happened to look right at me, they wouldn't know I was there.

As we waited, I indulged in my compulsive habit of checking my stats.

Name: Vivian Valesh

Race: Human
Class: Thief
Subclass: Shadow
Level: 46, 24% toward next level
Hit Points: 1250, Mana: 120
Attributes:
Strength: 37
Agility: 46
Constitution: 40
Wisdom: 15
Intelligence: 15
Charisma: 20
Main Skills: (Level 3 or greater)
Archery: Level 8, 82%
Acrobatics: Level 3, 56%
Climbing: Level 7, 22%
Dodge: Level 7, 12%
Parry: Level 6, 58%
Sneak: Level 8, 12%
Swords: Level 9, 73%
Minor Skills: (Under level 3 - Select to view)

Like most players using a sub-class, I didn't have that many main skills. Of course it made sense to focus on the skills you used the most, but I was now at a point where nearly all seven of my main skills were difficult to increase, save for Acrobatics.

I started to consider bringing up some of my sub-level 3 skills particularly ones that would allow me to use different weapons better, like Maces or Axes. One thing I was really keen on, though, was increasing something that would help farm better materials for crafters. There was good money to be had in nearly all crafting professions with practitioners desperate for mats to use in creating their wares.

One skill I'd idly toyed with the idea of raising was Herbology.

Herbology Skill

Is the study of basic plants and fungi. Advancement in this skill allows for the ability to effectively cultivate various flora.

Mine sat at Level 1 with 25% progression. I barely used it at all, mostly because I was too busy tromping over plants instead of picking them. But if I could raise it enough, I could start to find ingredients to sell on the market.

As I idly perused my skill numbers, I suddenly noticed movement ahead of me. Looking, I was surprised to see a large turtle lumbering in my direction. It was a pet of one of the players and it seemed to be exploring its surroundings.

The animal was as large as an overturned bathtub, with thick stubby legs extending from its sides. Steel spikes bristled from its huge shell which had been fused with segmented metal plates across its surface. No doubt the beast was used for engaging enemies and keeping their attention while its owner attacked from a safe distance.

The thing trundled about, checking the walls and lowering its head to the floor, sniffing. Could it smell me? As its explorations got closer to where I sat, I tensed up, ready to move. The little tank got closer, and I suddenly felt the illogical urge to see how close it could get.

Turns out, really close. The turtle came within two paces of me, its neck stretching outward with its head to sniff the air.

My heart was beating wildly. I needed to move. If I did it slowly, it wouldn't see me. But I found myself sitting there like a fool, drunk on adrenaline.

Its head angled close enough that if I reached out, I could touch it.

"Hey!" Someone called out.

Both me and the turtle turned to look.

One of the players, a gnomish archer, was glaring at the turtle. "Get back here," he said, his voice stern.

The huge turtle turned its body and moved toward its master, the large spikes on its shell nearly grazing the edge of my cloak.

Both gnome and turtle-tank returned to the group.

I exhaled, my heart rapidly pounding in my chest. That had been strangely exhilarating. But I knew I'd been stupid. Why risk everything I'd worked so hard for just to throw it all away for a cheap little thrill like that? What was I thinking?

Before I could consider this age old argument, the players of the group began to stand and organize themselves. It was time for the big show.

Shaking my head at my own stupidity, I waited and watched.

The guild leader gave a quick pep-talk about how great they all were and how they'd earned the right to be here at this final encounter. They would be victorious and the world would know how great they were when they defeated Xorrox. Blah blah blah. It was all for show. He knew, as well as everyone else there did, that many wouldn't survive the fight. But it was the risk they were willing to take for the glory of their annoying guild.

Finished with his little speech, the leader walked through the huge doorway and into the vast chamber beyond. The rest of the group quickly followed behind, chatting nervously to each other in excited tones.

I was in no hurry to follow. This was the end of the line and there was no where else they could sneak off to where I could lose them.

As I casually walked to the entrance, a work message suddenly popped up at the corner of my screen. I blinked at it, not expecting to be disturbed so soon since logging in.

The message said that the Icestation was beginning to shift to a new location and requested that I be present to supervise.

I almost laughed. Me? Supervise? That wasn't even in my job description. I was at the station simply for the company to exploit an insurance loop hole. As long as a human was present, they could operate without a specialized license, or some nonsense. I'd never been clear on the details. I was just happy to have a paying job that allowed me to delve into UFW all I wanted.

Frowning at the strange request, I dismissed it. The station AI could take care of things as it always did. It didn't need me as a glorified cheerleader.

I moved to stand within the doorway. Beyond was a vast rocky chamber with high vaulted ceilings. Rivulets of lava snaked down the walls to vanish into cracks around the floor's edges.

On the opposite side stood a giant humanoid demon. Its massive arms and legs were manacled with chains to the floor and the wall behind it. Long, curved horns sprouted from its huge head, each the length of a tree. Its skin was blood red and its eyes glowed a bright yellow.

Xorrox.

The players had assembled themselves opposite this captive terror, with fighting classes in the front, and magic casters and range attackers behind them. Standard group formation for practically every group encounter since the dawn of MMO gaming.

Xorrox glared at the group, snorting steam from huge nostrils and stomping its cloven hooves on the ground.

The great demon spoke, and the room boomed with its voice. "Who has come to my prison?"

The leader of the group came forward, a tiny gnat compared to the monster before him. "We have, foul creature!"

"To free me?" Xorrox shouted.

The leader shook his head, his helmet reflecting the light. "You're imprisonment is too lenient a punishment for your terrible crimes. We have been tasked by Grenwall the Great to destroy you once and for all."

Xorrox sneered. "You think you can destroy me, petty insects? What courage does it take to attack one who is bound?" The demon suddenly strained against the large chains which held it.

"Prepare to be sent back to the sewers of Hell, demon!" The leader shouted.

All of this dialog was according to script, with little deviation. Once finished, the first stage of the encounter would begin.

The leader shouted an order and the archers and mages attacked. Arrows and spells hit the demon across its body, and it roared in anger. Then, a large contingent of the fighters ran forward and assaulted its legs.

Xorrox roared and stomped and steamed.

For my part, I leaned inside the doorway and watched, mildly bored. My research showed this was the easy part. Once enough damage had been done to Xorrox, he'd be free of his bounds and attack the group wholeheartedly. Then I'd get a clear idea whether this whole endeavor had been worth my while.

Sure enough, Xorrox broke the chains, doing so one at a time for dramatic effect. All the while the players buffeted the demon with all they had. The more damage they could do now, the better.

Freed, Xorrox swung the mighty chains hanging from its wrists and dashed away several players to the ground.

The fighting continued. Xorrox smashing with his chains and using a breath of flame attack, and the group using every available offensive tactic in their arsenal. All the while, clerics cast heals and archers fired their bows.

The hours passed. Inch, by agonizing inch, Xorrox's health bar diminished. I took this time to surf the forums and check the latest Stelar News updates. I even considering slipping out of my suit to go grab something to eat, knowing I wouldn't miss much, but the risk was too great, so I stayed.

Eventually, after a lot of damage was given and received, Xorrox was defeated. The great demon collapsed to the floor in a massive heap and was still. The surviving members of the group cheered and gave each other hugs and high-fives.

I perked up. Time for my part in this little drama.

A huge treasure chest materialized before Xorrox's body, and the group cheered again. With its lid closed, one could only guess at the wonders it contained. But I knew one specific item it did have.

The black knight leader stepped toward the chest. This was my cue.

Still in Shadow form I darted along the wall of the chamber, mindful of the lava that cascaded down its surface.

The leader gave another speech, something about their guild's greatness, and how victory would always be theirs. Etc. I didn't care, my focus was getting as close to him as possible.

Once I'd reached the back of the chamber, and positioned behind the splayed body of the demon, I moved inward. Slinking across the floor, I came up to Xorrox's corpse which completely blocked anyone's view of me. On the other side I could still hear the leader jabbering on. Carefully, I edged around one huge horn and peeked.

The leader's back was to me, the closed chest beside him. Here I could plainly see all the faces of the players watching him with naked avarice. They wanted their share of the treasure, but had to wait for it first. Such were the rules of being in a civilized guild.

My heart was pounding in my chest. I was effectively standing in front of all these high level players. As soon as I moved in front of them, they would see me, Shadow form or not. But I had a trick up my sleeve, or should I say, Cloak.

The leader finally ended his agonizing spiel and turned to the chest.

Here we go, I thought. But I needed to wait. I couldn't act until the chest was actually open.

The leader placed his hand on the chest's lid, caressing it. "We worked hard for this, my friends," he said. The maudlin words sounding sickly to my ears. Hurry up and open the thing!

As I waited on pins and needles, coiled to spring, a pet broke from the group and wandered in my direction. Alarmed, I saw the stupid turtle-tank walking toward me.

Uh oh.

"And this," the leader said, patting the chest. "This is our just reward!" He opened the lid. Within was a large number of loot items which stuck out of a massive amount of gold coins. The chest overflowed with them.

Everyone leaned a little forward to get a better look.

The turtle was coming right at me and was several paces away. I was convinced it had sensed me somehow, but couldn't worry about that now.

Thanks to my Cloak of Shadows, I had the level one ability of pure Invisibility. Unlike my Shadow form, which could under the right circumstances be detected, Invisibility was absolute. But I was limited to a single duration of 30 seconds at a time.

Now was that time.

I activated my Invisibility and bolted forward. Running down the length of Xorrox's corpse, and crossing the view of all the oblivious players, I charged to the chest.

To my chagrin, the leader reached in and plucked out an item. The coiled snake statue!

He held it up for all to see. "This will give one of our special teams access to the Emerald Caldera, and its incredible loot!"

A changed my tactic and ran at the leader. As he continued speaking, I skidded to a stop next to him, and using both hands, grabbed the statue.

Instantly, my Invisibility canceled out. To the watching players, I suddenly blinked into existence beside their leader, both of us holding the statue.

Before anyone could even react, I wrenched the statue from the dark knight's grasp. "Thanks!" I said.

You have acquired an item: Statue of Sisorian (1 of 2) This statue is required to gain access to the Emerald Caldera instance. Can only be used once.

Value: Unknown.

The leader's head snapped around to look at me in surprise, but I was already sprinting away in the other direction.

Shouts of alarm and the sounds of spells being cast filled the air. But I had my back to it all as I race around the other end of Xorrox's corpse. As I ducked behind a cloven hoof, an arc of lightening blistered the ground beneath my feet. I jumped away, taking damage. One of the spellcasters had been on their toes. I cursed my bad luck.

Knowing I had only seconds, I fished through my pockets.

From around a massive hoof came the turtle-tank. Its expression could almost be described as one of affirmation, finally finding the intruder it had sensed all along. It motored at me with alarming speed, its stumpy feet thumping at the ground.

I finally pulled out the item I was looking for. A Teleport Token.

Then, a moment before the turtle could charge into me with its spikes, I pressed the token.

My last image was of the turtle's beaked mouth lunging for me, and huge spikes thrusting at my face.

Then the world dissolved away.

CHAPTER THREE

In an instant, the hot vaulted chamber of Xorrox's demise was replaced by the interior of an empty tavern.

Rows of wooden tables and stools filled the room, and a large hearth sat in one corner with a roaring fire. There weren't any patrons present, and in this place, there never was.

"Well, isn't it a surprise to see you again," a cheery voice said.

I turned around to look at the bar, its surface highly polished. Standing behind it was a plumb man with a bald head, with a long beard which extended down past his round belly.

"Good to see you, too, Fenwick," I said with a smile. My pulse still raced from nearly getting killed. I looked at the snake statue in my hand, its ringed coils twinkling like black diamonds. "In fact, I'm more than happy, I'm ecstatic."

Fenwick's ever-present smile grew. "Well, in that case, how about an ale? Got a new cask in of that butterscotch brand you like."

I slipped the statue into by pack. "Maybe some other time, Fenwick. I'm meeting someone at the Trading Post."

"It's on the house."

"In that case, pour me a mug," I said walking over to sit.

As Fenwick tipped a large mug under the spout of a fat cask, I sent Shwenn a quick text message.

Got it. Let's meet now.

Fenwick placed the frothing mug in front of me and went back to wiping down the bar-top with a cloth. Without any other customers, it was his default action.

Shwenn responded immediately.

You got it???

Yup.

Be there in five.

I smiled at Fenwick and downed the ale. It was exceptional. My simulation suit allowed for taste, but not the effects of any alcohol. Still, it didn't detract from how good the ale was. Also, sitting in the tavern and drinking helped my hit points regenerate faster. That lightning attack had hurt.

I pondered my day so far. I'd done it. After all that work, and all that risk, I managed to steal the statue without getting killed. And now I could look forward to possibly dying again, but this time in the Emerald Caldera.

"I take it things are well with you, Miss Valesh," Fenwick said, noticing my grin, his great beard shaking as he spoke.

"Could not be better, Fenwick. I am one happy lady, right now."

The barkeep nodded and turned to rub his cloth against some very clean mugs. The Teleport Token had been given to me by Shwenn, as part of our deal. They're horrifically expensive because they're horrifically useful. I'd keyed the teleport point on Fenwick and his empty bar, Fenwick's Folly. Its location was in the huge underground city of Crow's Fall in the Kingdom of Trendon.

Whenever I needed a safe place to teleport to, I always picked this place. Not just because the ale was wonderful, but because I almost always the only person to be there. Crow's Fall is packed with taverns, so much so that few, if any, people wandered through Fenwick's doors. Which suited me just fine. If I'm teleporting from somewhere, it's because I'm in a big hurry, or escaping certain death. Dealing with a crowd immediately after is jarring.

I downed the last of the delicious ale and stood. "Thanks, Fenwick, that was great." I slapped a gold piece on the bar.

Fenwick's eyes widened. "It's free, miss. And besides, this is too much."

"I had a very good day, today. Keep it."

The barkeep's smile widened as he slipped the gleaming coin into a shirt pocket. It would be the most he'd made in weeks.

I pushed my way through the front doors to stand outside in the street.

The nearby buildings were all desolate, or abandoned and boarded up. No one was about, not even a pickpocket. The street was barren of any people or potential customers. Another reason why Fenwick's Folly never got any business. It was in a crummy location.

I could see the city's massive domed ceiling high above, like a stone sky. Compared to the lava chamber this was a dream.

I headed down the street in the direction of the Trading Post which was close to the middle of the city. Curious as to what might be happening with Try And Catch Us at that moment, I set my avatar to auto-path and brought up a translucent net screen.

The guild was raging on the forums and various chat feeds. They'd been robbed and were seeking retribution. Despite the fact they still had everything else in Xorrox's loot chest, it was the statue that really ticked them off the most.

Soon, they posted a reward for the identity of the Shadow that pilfered their hard earn gains. I idly scrolled through the different names people offered as potential suspects. UFW is huge, with billions of players. Of which a sizable chunk of that population are Thieves and Shadows. So the list of candidates grew long. My name hadn't come up, yet, but I didn't doubt it wouldn't take long for them to figure it out.

Then things would get interesting. Hopefully that would only become a problem after I'd gone to the Emerald Caldera.

I was so engrossed with the guild drama sprayed over my screen, I didn't notice my avatar stopping outside the Trading Post.

Switching back to full control I looked around at the people milling outside the building, a large warehouse-like structure. I didn't see Shwenn, so I went inside.

The Trading Post was a large empty room which, at first glance, didn't appear to serve any real purpose. In fact, it was one of the most secure places to conduct business in the entire game. Once you passed through the doors of a Trading Post, no one could steal from you, or harm you, or pull any tricks.

Its large interior was lined with rows of small tables. Each designed to secure a trade or transaction without any chance of someone being ripped off. To add to this security, once you activated a table for a trade, a large tent sprouted around it, masking your activities from prying eyes.

Several tents dotted the floor, but the vast majority of the tables were empty. Again, I looked for Shwenn but didn't see her, so I walked to a nearby table and sat down in one of its plush chairs. The cost to use the transaction table was only a silver piece and many traders, and nervous players, swear by their usefulness. Before the Trading Post's existence, everyone had to trade by hand and hope for the best. Now, this facility could be found in every major city across the entire gaming universe.

After a few minutes, I began to worry about Shwenn. She was late. But as I was about to send her a chat request I saw here burst through the doors. I waved, and she hurried over.

"Sorry I'm late," she said, dropping into the opposite chair. "I was caught up in all the drama online."

Shwenn was an Elven Fire Mage and looked the part to a tee. She had long pointed ears that stretched past the back of her head, dark coffee-colored skin common for her Southern Islands race, and huge silver eyes. Her snow-white hair was cropped to her scalp and her chin narrowed to a point.

She wore a long blood-red robe which went to the floor and covered her hands. Its high collar was actually a row of flames that flickered around her neck.

Now I see why she keeps her hair short, I thought.

I said, "Yeah, Try And Catch Us has really got a bee in their bonnet now. They've been blasting the feeds the second it was over."

"What? No, I mean with my Caldera group. They're so excited that were going now it's taking all my energy to get them organized. Kind of like trying to herd kittens."

She folded her hands on the table and leaned over. "So, the statue."

I glanced around. "I think we should use a privacy tent for this, don't you?"

It took to the count of five before she realized I was suggesting she paid the one silver piece to get things started. There was no way I was going to pay, no matter how cheap it was. I had the statue after all.

Shwenn blinked as if she'd just had her flaming collar doused with water. "Oh, right! I forgot. Silly me." She fished out a silver coin from a fold in her cloak and placed it on the table.

The coin vanished and a tent suddenly materialized around us. Fire sconces hung by chains from overhead beams, and its walls of fabric undulated pleasantly as if caressed by a breeze.

Satisfied, I brought out the statue. The carved snake twinkled in the fire light and I noticed its eyes were little gray diamonds.

Shwenn's eyes lit up with excitement. "Oh. Oh, wow. It's identical to the other one, only this is red in color."

"What's the other one?"

"Kind of a sandy shade." She held out her hands as if ready to take an infant.

"Uh, first things, first," I said, a little perplexed. "We need to get this in writing."

Shwenn's face collapsed into one of confusion, "Writing? As in a contract?" The words came out of her mouth like shards of broken glass.

"Yes, as in a contract. Iron clad. Unbreakable. That kind of contract."

I watched her reaction carefully. For her part, she kept her expression frozen in a mask of surprise. I couldn't be entirely sure she'd keep me in the Caldera group, high honor score or not. Once she had the statue, she could simply not send me an invitation. But I wasn't going to let that happen. The potential end reward for me was too great.

Shwenn quickly regained her composure. "Well, okay, then. Not a problem for me. I intended to keep to our agreement, but if you need it locked, then lets do it."

We both nodded, and I placed the statue in a small square on the table before me.

Shwenn said, "Group contract." A parchment appeared in the square in front of her.

"Let's make it item specific. As in this statue."

"Very well," she said, her face neutral. "Item Specific contract, please."

A different parchment appeared, replacing the old on. She read it over and scribbled on it with a quill which appeared in her hand.

Finished, she slid the contract over to me. It basically stated that whatever quests or instances which are produced by using the snake statue, I, Vivian Valesh, would have a reserved slot in whatever groups participated in them.

Now, if she tried to use the statue to gain access to the Caldera, she couldn't without my being present. This was the security I needed. Words can only go so far in this game.

"Perfect," I said. "Thank you."

With a tight smile, she placed the parchment back in her square. A prompt appeared before me.

Accept Item Specific Contract Agreement? Y/N?

I selected yes. The same prompt appeared before Shwenn and she agreed, not that I expected any surprises at this point.

Suddenly, the parchment and statue changed position, switching sides. Shwenn scooped up the statue with both hands and cradled it to her chest. "Oh, it's been too long in coming. This is going to be great."

"If we don't end up dead, sure," I said putting the contract into my pack. The agreement was locked into the game itself, the copy I had was simply a reminder. But one I now coveted.

Shwenn smiled. "Oh, don't worry too much. I've got a great crew put together and we should sail right through it."

Uh huh, I thought, a little taken aback. Sail through the Emerald Caldera? Was she touched in the head or something? "So, when do we go?"

"Oh, tomorrow morning," she said, tucking the statue into her robes. "Here's the location and time." She sent me the info, and I looked it over.

"Helto Port? That's not too far from here. Like a twenty minute airship ride." I looked at the time set for the meetup. "Fourteen hours from now. Cool." It would give me time to get to Helto and then log off for a good night's rest. I'd certainly earned it.

"I'll see you there," she said, the tight smile returning. "Don't be late." Then she nodded and rushed off through the tent flap and was gone.

It was then I realized that she may have had the intention of backing out of the deal, all along. But now she couldn't. I felt a little disappointed. Finding honest players in the game was next to impossible. Since everyone wasn't technically themselves, they felt they could act like jerks if it served their purpose.

Still, I had my spot and nothing could stop that.

I pulled up my quest log and checked the one at the top of my priority list.

Locate the Shadow Blade

Somewhere on the mist-shrouded island of the Emerald Caldera is the rumored hiding place for the Legendary weapon, the Shadow Blade.

Secreted away there by the Mage Lords of Darkness centuries ago, it is considered impossible to find. Gain access to the Emerald Caldera and retrieve the Shadow Blade.

Reward: Shadow Blade (Legendary Set Item).

This was why I went through everything in the first place. Getting the statue got me a spot going into the instance. Once there, I'd have a chance to find the greatest Shadow Class sword that has ever existed.

I smiled to myself. This went better than I hoped. Now all I needed to do was not get killed on the Caldera and things would be great. Of course, given the savage reputation of the island, I knew that would be a tall order.

Leaving the Trading Post, I entered the street and pushed into its growing crowds. The difference between this area of the city and where Fenwick's Folly was located was stark. I made my way through its clogged avenues to one of the exit tunnels and eventually made it outside.

Crow's Fall was effectively under a large dome of rock, which resembled an overturned soup bowl. It had withstood wars and cataclysms, and had even being fully submerged in the ocean, once. Despite its trials over the centuries, it showed little sign of damage or weathering.

I followed the road through the strip of buildings that clung to the side of the dome. Past them was an airship station which had a regular route running to Helto Port every twenty minutes.

A quick stop at an item vendor to offload the items I picked up, netted me 178 gold pieces. I kept the health shot potions since I'd be needing them. Not wanting to miss the next airship, I hurried on.

As I climbed the stairs up to the platform, I could see the airship approaching. My plan when arriving in Helto was to stock up with much needed supplies then log off. My gold was meager, but I had enough to get the bare essentials; specialized arrows, potions and maybe rent a temporary defensive pet, like a turtle-tank. Anything that might help keep me alive long enough to find the Shadow Blade.

The airship pulled up to the platform, and its passengers disembarked.

Suddenly, the world shook and my vision tilted. When the shaking passed, I blinked in surprise and looked about. No one else reacted to the violent movement. Then it happened again, and I nearly pitched over. To my horror, I realized the shaking wasn't happening in the game.

A red warning message appeared on my screen. The station AI was demanding my presence immediately. Something had gone wrong with the station move.

Shocked, I quickly ran onto the airship, brushing past passengers. My mind raced. I had to log off, and quick. Looking for a safe place, I ran down into the hold and climbed through its stacks of crates.

The red warning message flashed angrily, and it wouldn't allow me to dismiss it. This was bad. This was really bad.

Finally, I found a large trunk in the back, half full of clockwork parts. I climbed inside and closed the lid above me.

As my vision shook again, and the station AI resorted to feeding a ringing alarm into my ear phones, I had only one thought as I quickly logged off.

Whatever it was that was happening in the real world, it better not mess up my chance at the Shadow Blade!

CHAPTER FOUR

As I pulled off my visor, I was assaulted by trilling alarm bells, and flashing red lights on the walls of my office.

Through the viewport I could see the jagged horizon of Callisto which had changed dramatically since I'd last looked only a few hours earlier. The scheduled move had taken place, but appeared to have hit a problem.

As if to emphasis it, the room shook again, and I was yanked around in my simulation suit's suspension cords.

"Wow," I said. That can't be good. As I hurriedly slipped off my suit I called out to the station's AI. "Abe, what's going on?"

"The station has encountered a fissure which has destabilized section fourteen to eighteen," a male voice said from everywhere and nowhere. The AI sounded incredibly calm, all considered, but it was programmed to be that way.

Free of my suit, I rushed to the workstation's terminal in the corner. Its screen showed an overlay of the massive station, which had the appearance of an octopus with fat, spiky tentacles.

Sections of several of the tentacles, referred to as arms, were flashing red. Scanning the data, it looked like several structural breeches had rendered parts of the station inoperable.

"This looks bad, Abe. What happened?"

"As the station transited over the rock plain toward Theta Point Eight, a tremor occurred. The strata beneath cracked open, pulling several sections apart."

The overlay showed the outline of the fissure which snaked under four of the station's arms.

Cold fear ran up my spine. "Abe, can we move away from the fissure? Are we at risk of falling in?"

"Unknown at this time. I'm working to reinforce the damaged areas before making an attempt to move."

I stared at the screen in horror, envisioning the huge station plummeting into the dark Jovian crevasse. Feeling hopeless, I asked, "So what can I do to help?"

"Nothing. But I am required to advise you to exit the station immediately. If the fissure worsens the station could be lost."

Leave the station? I looked back out at the cold, dark wasteland of Callisto with trepidation. In the entire time I'd been here, I'd never once suited up and gone outside. There hadn't been a need to. Until now.

Without thought, my eyes went to the simulation suit, hanging by its cords in the corner. What about the game?

Another quake, this one minor, shook some sense into me. "Okay, Abe. Get me out of here. What should I do?"

"Follow the main hallway down to the central radial, then descend to Drone Bay 6. Please use the stairs as the elevators are too risky at this time."

"Drone bay? What about the escape shuttles?" I was already moving down the hallway.

"Unless a complete failure of the station is imminent, use of the shuttles is not authorized per your contract clause 186 point 25, sub-paragraph nine."

"You mean I have to be on the verge of death to fly out of here?" I reached the outer radial at the center of the station and ran down a wide spiral staircase.

"Escape shuttles are expensive property of IceTech Industries and are only meant to be used in times of catastrophic danger."

Another quake sent me crashing into a wall, and I fell down several steps. I sat up in a daze. "This isn't catastrophic enough?" Pushing myself to my feet, I kept going.

"No, it is not," Abe said, not bothering to elaborate. His voice was pleasant but business-like. "Please continue to the Drone Bay 6."

"I am!" I said, reaching the station's lowest level and running down another hallway. Several wide doors lined the walls with signs of the various bays.

I entered the door marked Drone Bay 6. Inside was a small room with several chunky space suits hanging on the wall to one side. On the other was a wide viewport showing the main drone concourse. Dozens of drones were zipping about in all directions; diggers, loaders, trucks, analyzers. Their variety was almost unlimited, depending on the needs of the station.

Not wanting to be told, I began shoving myself into one of the suits. It felt like a giant, puffy sleeping bag crammed inside a bulky exoskeleton.

"How much air does this thing have?" I said as the tinted helmet automatically attached itself with a click. A loud hissing sound indicated pressurization.

"More than enough," Abe said. "Please don't worry."

"I am worried, Abe, this is scary as all hell!" I said. Unlike the fear I'd felt sometimes in the game, this was all too real to the point of being overwhelming.

"You'll be fine if you follow my instructions," Abe said. "Please approach the side airlock."

A small door was set into the wall marked Airlock 6. As I stood in front of it, my helmet panel blinked to life. I could see my air reserves and it didn't look great. But I held my tongue and tried to calm my nerves. Abe wouldn't let me die.

A horn blared and the airlock's inner door slid open revealing a tiny room.

"Please enter the airlock," Abe said.

"Shouldn't I grab a reserve canister?" I said looking for a small rectangular blue box. Weren't there supposed to be extras near the suits?

"That will not be needed. Now please enter the airlock."

Another shake practically sent me flying inside. The inner door slid shut, and I leaned against a wall. My heart was pounding in my ears and my breath was rapid and deep.

"Please calm yourself, Vivian," Abe said. "You may cause yourself to faint and I would be unable to assist you if that happened."

"Easy for you to say," I said, but I made an effort to slow my breathing. A hard job to do when you're about to step out into a radioactive nightmare.

Jupiter was a radiation belching monster that bathed its moons with the deadly energy. Being tidally locked, the side of Callisto that faced away from the planet was where Icetech and other companies conducted their operations. Although not being directly hit, there was still plenty of deadly radiation on this side of the moon. The station protected me from that. But now I was about to leave that protection.

"Once you are outside, there will be a digger waiting for you. Please enter its crew cabin on the left side."

"Wait? A drone? Shouldn't I be using a buggy? They're designed for people, ya know!"

"That is only one of the buggy's functions. Currently, all are being used to help with the repairs. This digger is all I can provide at this time."

Damn. The diggers used to be controlled by a crew years ago before full automation made their jobs redundant. Diggers were not known for their comfort.

"What about the gravity?" I asked. The station's grav-plates easily simulated a one G pull. But once I stepped outside, I'd be bouncing along with a tiny fraction of that.

"You'll be fine, Vivian. Now please, prepare for depressurization."

A light flashed within the airlock, and a warning sound beeped from my helmet's chin-deck. I grabbed a handle on the wall and braced.

The was a loud hissing which quickly faded, and I knew there wasn't any air left anywhere around me except in my suit. Then the outer door slid open, revealing a rocky, icy landscape.

"Where's the digger?" I asked, hesitant to step out.

"It's parked to your right. Please exit the airlock."

Sighing in exasperation, I stepped outside. Immediately to my right, parked within a recess in the station's lower bulkhead, was a digger drone. The huge array of claws and metal teeth on its front reminded me of some kind of mutant dragon.

I moved toward it. The change in gravity was immediate, causing me to slow my pace. It felt like a swarm of butterflies were bouncing inside my stomach.

Reaching the digger, I noticed a line of handles up its side, leading to a port door. It was at least two stories high. Cursing my suits bulk, I climbed. "What's the status?" I asked, while slowly ascending.

"Nominal at the moment. The fissure appears to have ceased expanding, but that could only be temporary."

Finally reaching the port, Abe triggered it open, and I climbed inside. As the door silently closed behind me I took in my new surroundings. Several high-back chairs and a darkened console amounted to all the exciting detail of the tiny space.

"Okay, now what?" It felt like I was in an abandoned shuttlecraft from decades past.

"Please connect your suit to the joint valve at the bottom of the console. That is the air supply."

I found the valve, but had to sit in one of the chairs to connect it. In moments a green light flashed on my chin-deck indicating a fresh supply of air was now circulating through my suit.

The digger suddenly jolted into motion, and drove a short distance from the station, then stopped.

With the air connected, I felt relieved and leaned back. "Okay. Done. Now what?"

"Now you must wait while I continue with the repairs."

I sat up in my chair. The Emerald Caldera! Quickly calling up a chronometer, I linked to my UFW account and queried how long before I had to meet Shwenn and her group.

It showed a little over twelve hours to go. I began to get nervous.

"Abe, how long will the repairs take?"

"I do not have an accurate estimate at this time, but I am working at maximum capacity."

"So it could take, say, more than twelve hours?"

"That is a distinct possibility."

I blanched. I couldn't miss the meetup. There was one particular restriction about the Emerald Caldera. Once an individual has both statues in his or her possession, they must activate the instance no later than two hours after sunrise the next morning. Which was why Shwenn wanted to meet when she did. The meetup was scheduled for three hours before the deadline, giving us time to reach the instance's gate. But if I didn't show up, the Emerald Caldera would lock us out for an entire year.

"Abe, when can I return to the station? I mean, I know it might not be fully repaired, but I'd still like to go back as soon as possible."

"I don't know, at the moment, Vivian. But I will inform you when it is safe."

"Please do so the second it is, please."

"I will."

I could only hope that I'd be able to log back in with time to spare. With nothing else to do, I leaned back in my chair and waited. Every minute felt like an hour, and I had to cancel the chronometer so I didn't have to see the seconds slowly pass.

My mind raced with all the terrible outcomes of my not being there to activate the instance, none of which were pretty. All the work I'd put into getting to this point would be wasted. Worse, I'd have to wait a full year before getting another chance.

The only positive was that even if we didn't use the statues now, I was linked to one of them and would still be needed as part of the next group going in. But I didn't want to wait that long.

Counting away the seconds in the cockpit was agonizing, and my nerves became fried. Part of my mind questioned why I'd be more concerned about an event in a game, than I was with the safety of the station. But I pushed those thoughts away. The station was out of my control. I was only an observer. In the game, I was a participant.

Cursing myself, I checked the chronometer again. Ten and a half hours to go before the meetup. There was no way I was going to stay sane waiting out that entire duration.

Sighing, I decided to use my suit's sleep inducement to pass the time and told Abe to wake me when the station was safe. Then I activated the sleep mode in my helmet and instantly drifted away.

I dreamt of falling through a giant fissure while frantically pressing at a Teleport Token. But the Token wouldn't activate, and I fell, and fell, and fell.

CHAPTER FIVE

I woke to a buzzing noise in my ears.

Sitting bolt upright, I blinked in confusion and looked around. The cockpit of the digger was the same. The only thing that had changed was the angle of the distant sunlight passing through its tinted view ports.

"You are awake?" Abe said.

"Yeah," I said trying to shake the cobwebs of sleep away. "What's happened? Is the station okay?"

"The situation has stabilized. I've managed to pull the station back from the fissure and am now continuing with repairs."

"Oh, thank God!" I said, and meant it. "Okay, can I return now?"

"I believe so, but please realize that some of the station's areas will be depressurized and inaccessible for a time."

Despite the pleasant warmth of my suit, I felt an icy shiver. "What about my work station?" And my simulation suit.

There was a slight pause, then Abe said, "I have just activated the atmosphere in that section. It may still be advisable to remain where you are until all repairs have been completed. But you may return whenever you wish."

I pulled up the chronometer, again. In red lettering it said -00:21.

I was twenty-one minutes late!

"I wish to go now!" I said, trying to stand, but my connection to the air valve yanked me back down. Mumbling curses I disconnected and went to the port door.

"Please wait a moment while I bring the digger closer to the airlock."

Why couldn't it have done this before? I thought to myself, watching the time tick away. Hanging onto the port handle I quivered with anticipation. I knew I was in trouble. Big trouble.

"Come on, come on," I mumbled to myself.

The digger backed up to its alcove in the bulkhead, and once the engine stopped a light on the port door blinked green. I pushed the door open, but the strange bulk of the suit made me pitch over and tumble out.

As I fell, grabbed onto the edge of the port's frame, my faceplate scraping against the digger's hull.

"Vivian, are you okay?"

I hastily grabbed onto the top rung and got my booted feet onto another. Taking a few seconds to calm my heart, I said, "Yup. Never been better."

"Please be careful, Vivian. There is no rush. The station isn't going anywhere for a while."

Descending the ladder, I almost laughed. The station wasn't what I was worried about. I was late for the single most important gaming instance since... Well, the last single most important gaming instance I participated in. But I was still late.

Reaching the ground, I ran to the airlock door, which meant I loped along under the low gravity.

As I practically flew toward the airlock, I said, "Open the airlock!"

"But you're not there y-."

"Open it now!"

"Very well."

The airlock door slide open just as I skidded to a stop, nearly falling over again. I scrambled inside and Abe closed it behind me.

I began to yank at my suit's helmet when a red light flashed on my chin-deck.

"Vivian, you cannot exit your suit until the airlock is pressurized."

The chronometer kept counting, -00:26.

"Then do it!"

The airlock fully pressurized, and the second my chin-deck flashed green, I pulled my helmet off.

"It is recommended to remove your suit once you are actually inside the station."

"Well, this is a new rule," I said, tugging off the suit arms. The inner airlock door slide open revealing the suit staging area.

Finally free of the thing, I raced out of the airlock and out into the hallway.

"Your suit is in the airlock, Vivian. Can you please return it to its rack?"

"Later!" I said, walking up the stairs. The sudden change to full gravity was agonizing. I felt like I weighed five hundred pounds. Each footstep took more effort than I though I could handle.

"Please do not over-exert yourself. Although you were not outside for too long, you still must give your body time to adjust to the station's gravity."

Plodding up the stairs and trying not to get angry at the universe in general, I asked, "Abe, do you have a mute option?"

"Of course."

"Then please mute yourself until I say otherwise. I need to focus, here."

"Very well," Abe said without a hint of reproach.

Finally reaching the top floor, I shuffled down the hallway and into my workstation area. The simulation-suit hung from its cords as if waiting for me.

But before I could even think of slipping into the suit, there was one all powerful duty I had to perform.

I used the bathroom. It had been many hours since I'd done so last and it couldn't be avoided.

Finished, I slipped into the simulation suit, and felt my body readjusting to the gravity a little more. Once I was fully hooked up, I logged back in, my heart pounding in my ears.

You have logged back into Unlimited Fantasy Worlds Online.

Enjoy the adventure!

My vision was dark, but my icons appeared at the edges of the visor. Realizing I was still in the trunk, I pushed open the lid. The view of the creaky airship's hold was a welcome sight.

As I jumped out and raced up to the deck, I checked the chronometer.

-00:42.

On the deck I found the ship in motion, traveling high over a forested landscape. Where was I? I checked my map and found the airship was heading back to Crow's Fall and was already a third of the way there. I realized my log out location in the trunk had been bouncing back and forth between Helto Port and the city over and over again. And I'd logged back during another return trip.

I was heading in the wrong direction.

An audio chat request appeared. It was from Shwenn.

Oh, boy, I thought as I accepted it.

Before I could even get a word out, Shwenn was shouting.

"Where are you? Do you know how long we've been waiting!" Her pleasant businesslike demeanor from earlier had vanished.

"Sorry!" I said. "I had a big RL issue that kept me offline. But I'm on my way now!" I looked around for a means to get off the ship. But my only option was to jump off and hope the fall didn't kill me.

"There is a very small window of opportunity here, Vivian," Shwenn said, her voice stern as a schoolmarm's. "And the time you're wasting is eating into it!"

"Yup, I know. Sorry. I'll be there as fast as I can." Suddenly, I noticed an airship approaching from the other direction. It was part of the same route and was going toward Helto Port. Watching it get closer, I realized the two ships would pass each other.

"When?" Shwenn said. She wasn't screaming, which I was a little grateful for, but incredibly annoyed. And I couldn't blame her. My situation was going to cost her, and everyone else involved, a whole year's wait. Unless I could get there quick.

"I'm on the airship now, and it's about to arrive."

Shwenn sighed, obviously trying to maintain her composer. "Okay, just get here quick. The others are really ticked off with you right now."

"I understand. And, again, I'm sorry-."

She cut the connection.

I didn't have time to feel any worse than I already did. The other airship was seconds from passing by, but looked like it would be a distance away.

Well, here goes nothing. With no other choice I backed up to the other side of the deck to get enough running room. Other players were milling about, some watching out of boredom.

I waited until the other airship was in position and then ran across the deck as fast as I could. It was a small distance, but I had to use every inch of it. Just as I started my run, a dwarven ranger walked across my path.

"Look out!" I shouted barreling right at him.

Surprised, the dwarf narrowly dodged out of the way, cursing at me.

I zoomed past and with my last step I used my Leap ability and jumped. Vaulting through the air, I sailed over the forest far below. My eyes were on the airship as it crossed my descent. It was going to be close.

I crashed onto the deck at full speed and tumbled into a roll. My momentum shot me across like a bowling ball and I smashed through the railing on the opposite side. Slipping over the side of the ship, I desperately grabbed at the edge of the deck while sticking my feet to the hull with my Sure Foot ability. Miraculously, I had stopped from falling.

Acrobatics skill increased! Level 3, 57%.

Careful not to lose my grip, I pulled myself up and onto the ship. I made it.

A handful of players who had witnessed my suicidal leap broke into applause. I bowed and brushed myself off.

I moved to the bow of the ship and looked toward Helto Port. It was still a fair distance away, but there was nothing else I can do about it. Other than this ship there was no way to get there faster. I even contemplated dropping to the forest below and then using Smoke to ride in, but the distance was far too great. Even with a health boost and my Freefall ability it would have meant a reroll.

Chagrined, I could only perch on the bow and stair at the small city as it grew a little bigger every passing moment.

I had forgone checking the chronometer and had to take solace in the fact that Shwenn knew I was coming. But that didn't stop me from feeling like a complete tool. There was nothing I could have done about the Icestation. It was an event well beyond my control which kept me from the game. But explaining that to her probably wouldn't go too far. All I could hope for is to get to her with enough time for the instance to be activated.

Within a few minutes the airship platform got closer. By now, my Leap had reset from its cooldown of three minutes and could be used again. And I did.

Even before we docked I did another run, this time along the length of the bow. At the edge, I used Leap and again I was airborne. This time, instead of crashing, I arced toward a grassy field in front of the platform. Just as I was about to land, I summoned Smoke.

The magnificent black steed appeared already in mid-gallop and I thudded onto his saddle. With a surprised laugh, I angled Smoke toward Helto's main dock where the group was to board a ship.

Cutting across the city, and charging through its streets like the Gods of Deletion were on my tail, I passed several vendor stalls. My original plan was to stock up before leaving, but that wouldn't be happening now. I was stuck with what little I had.

Finally, I rode off a street and onto the docks. There was a few fishing boats lined up along the water's edge, but only one large ship was present. That had to be the one.

As I rode Smoke toward it, I saw a tall dark-robed elf lean over the rail and wave. She then made motions for the captain to throw the lines.

In seconds I was racing up the side of the ship, but instead of stopping I had Smoke ride close to the dock's edge. I jumped from his saddle and collided with the ship's hull, grabbing onto a tangle of rigging as I bounced off.

You have suffered 60 hit points of crushing damage.

Seeing stars, I hung on for dear life, but I dismissed Smoke just as his momentum carried him over the end of the dock. He vanished in midair.

"Are you okay?" Someone called.

I looked up to see Shwenn looking down at me, her flaming collar fluttering against the buffeting wind. The ship had already pulled away from the dock and was making speed toward the deep ocean. I suspected the captain was using high level sailing abilities to take advantage of the wind. Within moments we were moving at an incredible clip.

I climbed up the rigging, my avatar still seeing little stars. Reaching the top, I pulled myself over the rail and hopped onto the deck.

Before me stood Shwenn along with four other players, an ogre, a human, a dwarf and a minotaur. All of whom were scowling.

After I'd had a second to recover, Shwenn said, "What happened? Do you realize how late you've made us? Do you understand how important this is?"

The dwarf said, "Can you get her grouped, first. At least we can get this locked into place." He was dressed in the billowing gray robes of a Cleric class.

"Yeah," said the big ogre, "Then you can berate her." His bare chest was zigzagged with the tattoos and body piercings of the Slayer sub-class. On his back was strapped a huge double-bladed axe.

Shwenn rolled her eyes and took a deep breath. "Very well, here."

You have been invited to group with Shwenn Brookblade. Join Accept/ Decline?

Feeling welcome, I accepted.

Appearing down the side of my view was a list of names of everyone in the group, each with a pair of bars, health and mana. Now I could see how each player was fairing without having to look directly at them.

Before anyone else could speak I raised my hands. "Look, sorry guys. I had a serious RL issue that was completely and totally out of my control. I had to log out on the airship to Helto and couldn't come back until now." I looked to Shwenn, "So, yes, I know how late I've made us and yes, I know how important this is." More so to me than them.

"See, that all sounds reasonable," the human named Witt said. He was a level 53 warrior, wearing a nifty set of ebony chainmail armor with twin longswords on his back.

Shwenn glared at me for a few more seconds then her expression softened. "Okay. You had us all tied up in knots thinking this was going to fail before it even started."

The dwarven cleric, named Grumm, level 50, stepped forward and shook my hand. "Great job getting the statue, by the way. I can't even imagine what it took to do it. Maybe you can tell me about it over an ale once this is over." I could see all his fingers and thumbs were studded with Attribute boosting rings.

"Yeah," I said taken a little aback by how everyone's demeanor had changed. "And I know just the tavern to go to."

"Done," Grumm said with a smile. His long black beard was well groomed and braided together with a half dozen talismans.

"I'm Bozar," the ogre slayer said, thumping his barrel chest with a meaty fist. He was level 52. "You royally ticked off Try And Catch Us, so for that you have my gratitude. Oh, and for the statue too."

"Don't like 'em?" I said.

"Bunch of stuck up FILTEREDs," he said. "Anyone who can take them down a peg or two is good in my book."

"Welcome aboard," Witt said. "Both the group and the ship."

Everyone turned to look at the minotaur, who still glared at me. He wore a matching set of brown leather armor with an array of daggers on his belt. After a few uncomfortable seconds, he broke his stare and looked at the others. "I hate to have to point this out again, but why do we need two thieves?"

Confused for a moment, I noticed his player information and nearly gasped. He was a level 50 thief! A Minotaur!

"Now we discussed this before, Holpa," Shwenn said. "We needed her to get the statue and a spot in the group was the price. Fair is fair."

Holpa shook his head. "Our group dynamic is gimped now, you realize that? Why couldn't she be something more useful, like another DPS casting class or even a proper ranger?"

This sounded like an old argument they'd been through before. For my part, I was still stunned at this guy's class choice for his race. He was huge, almost as big as Bozar. I couldn't imagine the size penalty he took trying to sneak around or use his Hide In Plain Sight ability. Maybe he did it as a joke at the start and never bothered to reroll. He was level 50, after all, so at least he made it that far.

"The group dynamic isn't gimped," Witt said, facing off with the minotaur who was nearly twice his size. "She's a shadow, not just a thief. And she's got a bow, too, if you hadn't noticed."

"Kill a lot with that?" Grumm asked me with a smile.

"More than my fair share," I said.

Holpa kept shaking his head, his long horns nearly reaching the sail rigging above him. "I think it's a waste."

Shwenn held up her hands. "Okay, enough of that. The group is what it is, and that's not going to change."

But Witt wouldn't let it go. "Why don't you say what's really bothering you, Holpa? Why you're really so upset."

Holpa scoffed and folded his arms, but he didn't respond.

Witt said, "You're upset because you didn't think you had what it took to go down into that dungeon and get the statue. That's what this is really about. We asked you over and over, and you wouldn't do it." He pointed a finger at me. "She had what it took, and now we're standing on this deck heading to the Emerald Caldera because of her. Not you. So if you want to talk about waste…"

Holpa bristled and took a step toward the warrior, and Witt responded by drawing his twin swords.

Shwenn jumped between them, looking tiny in comparison to them both. "Red light, boys! Red light! Now's not the time to FILTER in each other's faces. We have an instance to initiate so let's concentrate on that."

The two players glared at each other, and for several moments I was certain things were going to get ugly. But to my surprise, Holpa backed down, turned away and stormed off in a huff, his hooves clomping loudly on the deck.

The tension broke and everyone dispersed. I found myself sighing in relief.

Witt came over. "Quite the welcome, huh?"

"I've had better," I said. My brain was still recovering from the last hour, both in real life and in the game. "But I'm just glad to be here."

Witt's smile widened and for a moment I thought it bordered on lecherous.

As I was about to politely excuse myself from his hovering presence, a sailor called out from the crow's nest high above.

"Ship on our wake!"

We rushed to the rails and looked.

Sure enough, another ship was nearby and looked to be following us. Behind them was the thin line of the coast, and Helto Port. Our ship was making good speed, but the other was just as fast.

"Pirates?" I asked. I didn't think they would operate within view of a major port.

"Nope, not pirates," Witt said, frowning. "That ship is being operated by Try And Catch Us."

CHAPTER SIX

Crew men scrambled over the deck and along the rigging around the sails. The captain stood on the aft deck at the wheel, shouting orders. A quick glance told me he'd been hired because of the speed bonuses he could imbue onto the ship. I hoped it would be enough.

My new group crowded the rails of the aft deck to watch the Try And Catch Us ship get closer and closer.

"Man, they are almost flying in that thing," Bozar said. "Guess they hired a faster captain."

Witt shook his head, "Doubt it, we grabbed the best one we could find on the entire coast. My guess is they're using an item, or a relic of some kind."

Whatever it was, the other ship was gaining on ours.

I looked to Shwenn, who was staring at the ship with worry. "How long until we're where we need to be?" The instance had to be initiated at a place called Viper Rock within a certain time frame.

Tearing her eyes away, she pulled out a map which showed our ship's position relative to the coastline. Ahead was a small dot marked Viper Rock. "We're making great progress, all considered, so we should almost be there within the time window." She looked over the bow and at the distant blue horizon.

I looked, too, but could only see waves and clouds. Then as the ship rode down the crest of a large swell, a tall, rocky outcropping could be seen in the distance, jutting out the sea.

"There it is!" Shwenn said. But it was too far. The other ship would overtake ours long before we got there.

"Will we still have time?" I asked.

"For the instance to be initiated? We better, or this will be a really short trip." To the captain she shouted, "Are you at full speed, sir? Can you push her any faster?"

"Neigh, m'lady!" The captain said, his eye on a little telescope, looking to the outcropping. "I've given her all she's got! It's up to the Gods now!"

Never mind the gods, I thought. This all came down to player ability. I looked back at the other ship which was just at the edge of my bow range, for what good that would do. At best I may be able to pick off some its sailors, and maybe hurt some of the guild players, but nothing I could launch at it could stop its progress.

"Anyone else have bows?" I asked, hopeful for a little backup.

"I do," Bozar said, producing a beautiful longbow.

"Me, too," said Witt, a short bow made of dark cedar appearing in his hands.

Suddenly, the guild ship surge forward, creating a large cresting wave before it.

"How are they doing that?" Grumm said, aghast. "Are they hacking?"

The ship had drawn close enough that the crew and players on it could be seen in better detail.

Struck with a thought, I grabbed the captain's telescope, who protested.

"I just need this for a second, captain!" I said as I pointed it at the bow of the other ship and looked.

Their deck was filled with at least forty players, many of whom I recognized from Xorrox's encounter. Aside from looking very pleased with themselves, I could tell their bloodlust was up. They were on the verge of getting revenge and retrieving the statue. Both statues, actually, if they killed Shwenn, too, which they would.

Standing right at the point of the ship's bow, and leaning over the rail, was the dark knight leader. In his hands was a large figurine which he held before him. It was producing a misty energy that spread outward to enshroud the ship.

"Oh, snap!" I said.

"What? What is it?" said Shwenn.

"They're using a relic to speed up the ship. I can see it." The figurine kind of looked like a miniature Xorrox. No doubt, one of the loot items it dropped.

"Okay, so it's a legal hack," Grumm said, looking anxious. "What are we going to do? They'll board us soon."

The other ship was surging over the waves, but instead of seeing this as our fates being sealed, I saw it as the perfect opportunity.

"Here," I said to Shwenn, handing her the telescope and pulling out my bow. "Hold this."

"What are you going to do?"

"Something desperate," I said, without exaggeration. My special arrow stock was limit thanks to my inability to load up before all this. But none of them could be used, anyway, for what I was about to attempt.

I placed my feet shoulder width apart and locked them to the deck with my Sure Foot ability. This prevented the pitch and sway of the deck from messing with my aim.

Then I nocked a regular arrow in my bow.

"Are you going to try and play William Tell?" Witt asked.

"Gonna send a gift to an old friend," I said. I pulled the arrow back and aimed it high. Then I waited until just the right moment.

Encouraged by my showmanship, Witt and Bozar fired their bows, but their arrows fell short. But judging how fast the other ship was coming, it wouldn't be an issue for long.

I centered my focus on the figure of the dark knight. Then, finally satisfied with the range I shot the bow while combining two of my abilities at once; Sure Shot and Multi-shot.

Instead of one arrow launching from my bow, there were four, thanks to my level three Multi-shot. In a cluster, the arrows arced through the air toward their target.

I watched in anticipation as the arrows descended.

The other group didn't seem to notice the little volley coming their way, or just didn't care. What could we do to them, now?

But just before the arrows landed, a warrior suddenly lunged toward the leader, his shield arm reaching out.

At the moment of impact, the warrior's shield had crossed in front of the leader's face. Three arrows hit down the shield in a line. But the leader hadn't been my Sure Shot target.

The fourth arrow struck the Xorrox figurine, and it shattered. A small concussive wave blasted from the impact and everyone on the ship was sent sprawling to the deck, with one toppling overboard.

The result of the figurine being destroyed was immediate. Their ship suddenly slowed as if hitting a sand bar and came to a stop.

As I watched the ship pitch about under the sudden halt of its momentum, everyone on mine cheered.

"Wow! That was aces, Vivian," Witt said, patting me on the back.

"Thanks, but it was mostly luck." And a lot of high level abilities.

If any of the group were still uncertain about me before, they definitely weren't now. Even Holpa looked a little impressed.

Our ship tore away from the now dawdling Try And Catch Us vessel.

All eyes turned to the horizon at the bow. The outcropping was close enough to see it was a huge carved image of a snake, leaping from the sea. Its eyes twinkled like rubies under the ocean sun.

We rushed to the bow of the ship to look as we got closer to it.

"I don't see the gate," Grumm said. "Shouldn't there be one?"

"Not yet," Shwenn said. From the folds of her robes she brought out both snake statues, one red, the other light brown. She held them in front of her and waited.

"What happens next?" Bozar asked.

As if in answer, the ruby eyes of the huge statue in the ocean glowed, growing brighter and brighter.

Just as the ship passed in front of its arched head, a bright beam of red light shot out of its eyes.

The light struck both statues in Shwenn's hand, causing them to glow in turn. Then from their eyes shot out a beam of light over the bow and across the sea in front of the ship.

A massive travel gate suddenly appeared in the water before us, most of it submerged. It had to be the biggest one I'd ever seen in the game.

Through its massive portal could be seen another ocean. But unlike the calm waters around us, this one seethed and thrashed under violent stormy skies.

"Oh, boy," I said, watching sheets of wind and rain buffet the other side of the portal. "This should be fun."

"Looks dangerous!" the captain shouted from the aft deck. "Dare I take her in?"

The group chuckled. This was all part of playing the game. We'd just gained access to some of its most exclusive content. A little storm wouldn't stop us now.

"Take her in captain!" Shwenn said, still holding the statues up. Their light appeared to keep the gate activated.

Without any more delay the ship sailed forward.

I watched in awe as we past the terminus of the gate, its upper arc easily higher than our mast. In moments, we went from a relatively peaceful setting, to a realm lashed by mother nature.

As the ship heaved over waves, the travel gate's portal changed from showing us calm seas and blue skies, to a silver plane. We were all the way through.

The statues in Shwenn's hands ceased glowing and then cracked, crumbling to dust. As she tried to brush it off her hands the ship pitched and she grabbed onto the rails. "We did it!" She shouted over the howling wind.

I tried to give a thumbs up, but even with my Sure Foot ability active, I had to hang onto the rails, too. "Now comes the easy part," I said with a smile.

She tried to laugh but ended up with a mouthful of rain and coughed.

Everyone was hanging on for dear life as the sails flapped above. Some rigging came loose and crashed to the deck.

The entire horizon was consisted of huge slate colored waves, all jostling each other for a chance to swamp the little ship.

"Where's the island?" I shouted to Shwenn.

"No idea!" She said and turned to the captain. "Captain! Do you have a navigation point now for the island?"

As the captain was about to answer a small mast suddenly cracked overhead and fell on him, bringing down one of the sails.

Bozar and Witt managed to rush over and tried to move the heavy beam off of him. The wheel spun freely, and the ship pitched to the side.

Dodging rigging which swung about wildly, I grabbed the wheel. But when I looked ahead all I could see were the peaks of waves and dark clouds.

Shwenn stumbled over and grabbed onto my shoulder. "He was our only means of navigation. Can you sail?"

"No!" I shouted over the screaming wind. Its power made the rain feel like bullets. Holding the wheel steady, I kept looking for something, anything that might indicate land.

Someone shouted from above and I looked up. The sailor in the crow's nest was pointing about twenty degrees to the right of the bow. "Land! Land ho!" A horrific gale of wind suddenly ripped the sailor from his tenuous perch and zipped him from view to vanish overboard into the roiling chaos.

Mortified, I looked to where he'd pointed. As the ship pitched and heaved, I caught a glimpse of something between the waves. A mountain peak.

Then it was gone. Desperately, I spun the wheel hoping it was still functioning. The massive sail above me was stretched taught. Suddenly, a terrific ripping sound joined the cacophony. The main sail tore right down the middle, its remnants flapping in the wind.

I looked at the wheel in my grip and realized I wasn't steering anything. We were at the mercy of the storm.

Looking around to check on the rest of the group, I could see all of them were hanging on to whatever they could, to keep from being thrown into the sea.

My gaze landed on Holpa. The minotaur had wrapped his large arms around the inner banister that lined the inside of the aft deck. As rain drenched his face, I saw him snorting out water from his huge nostrils. His bovine eyes were staring at me with unabashed hatred.

That guy's got issues, I thought as I looked away. If I was going to die here, it wouldn't be while having a staring contest with such an admirer.

Cringing against the rain, I looked to the bow. The mountain peak appeared, again, but this time closer. Were we actually approaching land?

Suddenly, a huge wave crashed into the left side of the ship, heaving it upward. Riding its massive swell, I could see the mountain dip lower and I realized how high we must be.

Then the wave sent the ship downward. Anything not bolted to the deck slid to the side and more sailors were sent screaming into the sea.

A work message popped up in the corner of my screen.

"Not now!" I shouted into the raging storm. But instead of another warning requiring me to log off, it was a message from Abe. The station was now secure, and a new transit path was being calculated.

Wonderful, I thought, as I blinked the message away. That, at least, was something to be happy about.

Another large wave slammed into the side of the hull, sending the entire ship pitching over. But it turned out to be a blessing.

In moments, the ship instantly emerged from the terrible storm into calm seas again, as if passing through a curtain.

Bewildered, I looked about.

The ship had been dumped into a tranquil lagoon. Behind us was a wall of wind and clouds that still raged. Looking up I could see this angry wall extending hundreds of meters into the sky.

Instead of the screaming of the wind, a pleasant breeze carried the calls of seagulls and other sea birds through the air.

Carefully, I stood up on the deck. I noticed the wheel in my hand had shattered at some point and all I held was a broken piece.

Looking around at the group I found them trying to stand up, equally dazed.

Before us was a huge island with a mountain sitting squat on the far side. High ridges of rock extended outwards from either side of the mountain to encircle the island like arms, both ending at the edges of the lagoon. Within this embrace was a vast, dense jungle of the deepest green I'd ever seen.

The Emerald Caldera.

CHAPTER SEVEN

For several moments I took in the spectacle of the wall of storms which extended beyond view to either end of the horizon. Within, the violent hurricane-like weather could plainly be seen. But on this side of the wall it was like a holiday paradise.

Writt walked over to me, shoving rigging out the way. "I love this game!" He said with a smile. "Where else can you get a thrill ride like that?"

"I'd of been happy if we didn't go through that at all, thank you very much," I said, wringing out my Cloak. Being a Legendary item didn't make it storm resistant.

We looked over at a crescent-shaped beach that lined the lagoon.

"I think we're drifting," Shwenn said.

"Better than sinking," Grumm said, shaking the water out of his beard.

"No, I mean were drifting into those rocks!" she said pointing. The furthest edges of the lagoon were lined with breakers, and the ship was headed toward them.

Cursing under my breath I ran down the length of the ship, jumping over dead bodies and fallen rigging. At the aft deck I found the anchor perched on the deck's edge. A huge chain extended from it to vanish into a hole into the hold below. I looked around for what to do.

"Hurry!" Shwenn shouted.

What did she think I was doing? Lazing around?

I noticed a wooden lever in the deck next to the hole and grabbed it.

Drop anchor? Yes or No?

I selected Yes, and the lever yanked forward in my grip.

The anchor suddenly dropped from view and the thick chain moved. I stepped back and watched the chain clatter by with alarming speed. I heard the anchor splash and within a few moments the chain stopped.

Another message appeared.

Set anchor at this location? Yes or No?

Seemed like a great spot to me. I selected Yes.

Anchor set. Pull lever again to retract anchor when ready. Crewmen required 10.

I looked across the ruins of the ship's deck. Only three crewmen remained alive. That will be a problem for later, I thought.

The group assembled at the center deck, checking themselves over. Grumm moved to each one, giving heals as needed.

As he approached me, he touched my arm and smiled. "You're not too bad, but I'll top you up, all the same."

"Thanks," I said. Apparently, I'd taken some damage other than when I'd jumped for the ship, earlier. I gave Grumm's mini-profile on my group list a glance.

Grumm Darkstone, Dwarf Cleric, Level 50

Hit Points: 1,050/1050, Mana: 620/1,120

"Nice mana pool," I said, then nodded at the rings on his fingers. "Boosted, right?"

"To the moon," Grumm said, taking a mana potion from a side satchel and drinking it. Finished, he placed the empty vial back. "Saved people from many a reroll, including mine." He wiggled his fingers, their rings twinkling. "Wisdom and Intelligence is my addiction of choice. Can't save lives without the mana to do it."

"Do you have a weapon?"

"Do I?" he said with a grin. A large staff appeared in his hands. It was made of gnarled wood, varnished to a high sheen. The head piece was literally that, a head. It looked to be of a Satyr, its emaciated goat-like features made all the more menacing by the tipped points at the end of its curled horns.

"Here, check it out," Grumm said, and passed it to me.

You have taken an item: Staff of the Holy Goat

Required Intelligence: 35

Required Wisdom: 32

Damage: 120-185

15% Chance of Level 2 Knock Back on hit (Kick of the Goat)

+120 Mana

+25% Casting Efficiency

+15% to Healing Spells

+22% to Offensive Holy spells

Value: Unknown

Bound to Grumm Darkstone. Cannot be traded.

I let out a long whistle of appreciation. "Now that there is a staff. Where'd you get it?" I asked, handing it back. The desiccated eye sockets of the head seemed to be looking right through me.

"The Bredon Complex. It's a multi-stage dungeon in the Savage Wastes. Most of my group wiped there, but I managed to survive thanks to finding this staff when we were half way through it."

I wanted to know more, but Shween stood in the middle of the group and clapped her hands.

"Okay, everyone, attention please. Let's form a game plan before making landfall. As you know, the Emerald Caldera is a medium sized random instance. It's never the same twice, so all the information on it is mostly useless. But there is one constant every group has encountered before us."

"Snakes," Holpa said. "FILTERing hate 'em." It was the first words he'd spoken since his little tirade.

Shwenn nodded. "Right, snakes. The last boss will probably be a snake or reptile of some kind."

"What about the quests? They different, too?" asked Witt, fixing the talismans in his beard.

"Probably," Shween said. "Most likely we'll find someone in need of rescuing from a sacrifice or something, but we won't know yet. But all that is just preamble. What are we *really* here for?"

"Loot!" everyone shouted in unison.

I blinked in surprise and laughed. At least they had their priorities straight. And, it just so happened to be mine, as well.

Shwenn waved a hand at Bozar. "Bozar is the main tank. He'll use his Slayer's Battle Howl to keep the aggros interested in him."

Bozar produced a kite shield from his inventory, its wide surface was painted with a portrait of his own face, screaming. He wielded the double-blade axe in on huge fist and clanked it against the shield. To Grumm, he said, "Keep me juiced up, squishy, and I'll keep you alive."

Grumm held up a hand. "Sounds like all the motivation I need."

Shwenn continued. "Witt with be secondary tank, and chaser to draw any strays who can't get under control. Holpa, do your backstab thing whenever you can, but save the heavies for the tanks. For my part, I'll do my best to burn them all to ash."

She looked to me. "Vivian, since you've got mad bow skills, please act as our main range attacker unless things get too hot, then Shadow as you see fit."

"Not a problem," I said with a nod. It was good to be in a group that at least tried to set a plan of action before things got crazy. Whether it would stay that way remained to be seen.

Shwenn turned to survey the lagoon.

Both sides of the long crescent shaped beach ended at the rocky ledges that towered over the jungle. At its middle point was the beginning of a path into the thick vegetation. Two tall statues stood on either side of it. From my vantage point they looked to be a species of snakemen, with torsos on a long snake body, and armed with towering serrated spears.

"Bet those animate," Bozar said with a sniff. "Statues always FILTERing animate in this game."

Perched on a grassy mound, at the edge of the lagoon was a wide stone platform. Atop it sat what looked to be a massive conch shell as big as an ox.

Behind all this was the jungle, thick, green and seemingly impenetrable.

Witt pointed at the snakemen statues. "We need to land as far away from them as we can. Don't want any problems before we even get a chance to get out of the boat."

"Good point," Shwenn said. See looked around for the last three crewmen and pointed at two. "Prepare the landing boat, you can row us to shore." They snapped to attention and ran over to a small boat, hanging over the side.

To the third, she said, "You're the new captain, congratulations."

The crewman saluted and smiled. "Thank you, m'lady! I shall serve you honorably."

Shwenn said, "You can be as honorable as you like, just don't die before we return. Repair what you can and make sure no one tries to board or sink the ship. Without you, we can't get back."

The landing boat was lowered to the water, and the group gathered at the rail to climb down.

While I waited, I stared at the lagoon, trying to discern anything we may have missed. Looking at the statues I could tell they were going to be a nasty encounter.

I looked to the newly minted captain who was wrestling with a Gordian knot of rigging. "Does this ship have cannons?"

"No, m'lady! We're just a transport ship. No cannon to speak of."

"You didn't expect it to be too easy, did you?" Witt said from beside me. "If we blast 'em before they animate, then we can't loot 'em, or get xp."

"I'd rather increase our chances of surviving the landing first, then worry about missing out on all that."

I was the last one to climb down into the boat, and as I descended, I noticed Witt watching me intently, an oily grin on his face.

Oh, great, I thought as I dropped in. I made a point of sitting far from him as I could. No need to encourage him more.

We pushed off from the ship and the two crewmen dipped their oars into the water and rowed.

The massive storm wall towered over us, black clouds roiling inside. But everyone's focus was on the beach, and the snakemen statues.

Witt pointed at the furthest spot possible for us to land on. "Make landfall there. If those things come alive we'll hang back and kite them."

But what if they can swim? I thought. I readied my bow as did Bozar and Witt.

The lagoon crossing was uneventful, if not pleasant. The lush jungle was alive with sounds, birds called and monkeys chittered and howled. The distant mountain peak was barren rock, devoid of vegetation. I wondered what we'd find there.

The crewman brought the small boat to shore and jumped out to keep it from drifting. The group climbed out and splashed up onto the beach. The warm clear water came up to my waist as I jumped over and waded ashore. My eyes never left the statues, which remained still.

Everyone was also scanning the jungle treeline for any threats, but none presented themselves.

"Why aren't they attacking?" Holpa said, watching the snakemen. He was dual wielding a crystal dagger and a fan-tipped short sword with a glowing pommel.

"We ain't triggered them, yet," Bozar said, his head on a swivel. "Don't worry, you'll get your chance, soon."

After several tense moments, Shwenn looked to Witt, who nodded. She turned to the crewmen. "Take the boat back to the ship. Be ready to return to shore immediately if we signal you."

The two crewman saluted and then hurried to get the boat back into the water. Soon, their paddles beat at the lagoon waters faster than when they'd arrived. They were eager to be away from this place and I could share their apprehension.

Grumm pointed at the jungle. "What if we just head straight in there and go around those two? They look nasty."

"My guess is they're the beginning of the quest chain," Shwenn said. "They're the only thing here, after all."

"Except for that shell," Holpa said.

The huge conch shell was on the other side of the beach, behind the snakemen.

Bozar looked to Shwenn, "Your call, boss. I don't care which, just as long we don't stand out here any longer. We're too exposed."

"Okay," Shwenn said, "First lets get out any pets we have-."

A message suddenly appeared before my vision, and I could tell the others could see it as well.

Your party has discovered a mysterious island beyond the wall of storms. What secrets might it hide?

Welcome to the Emerald Caldera where death is almost guaranteed.

"Oh, what the FILTERED is this?" Bozar said, surprised.

Here are three random restrictions to increase the challenge of this instance.

Uh-oh, I thought. This won't be good.

Random Instance Restrictions:

1) No Mounts.

"Are you kidding me?" Holpa said. "We gotta walk this whole thing?"

2) No Teleport Tokens

This brought a chorus of groans of disbelief. Not that it mattered to me because I had none. But now there wasn't an easy path out of this place for those who thought they could just teleport away when things got too rough.

Shwenn held up her hands as everyone grumbled and cursed. "It's okay, we expected something like this. This has happened before to other groups, but not these two restrictions exactly. We just happened to get the short end of the stick."

I was nonplussed. Other than not being able to ride Smoke around, I wasn't bothered.

The message continued.

3) One Island Altering Event

Surprised, everyone held their breath in anticipation. What did that even mean?

Initiating event.

Suddenly, in the distance a massive explosion could be heard, and the sand shook beneath our feet. We all turned to look.

The mountain peak had exploded, thick smoke and rocky debris flew into the sky. From the resulting hole at its top belched glowing red magma which flowed down its side to vanish from view behind the jungle.

I stared at the volcano in stunned silence, its implications running rampant through my mind. We had to contend with an active volcano, too?

The message continued.

Enjoy the added challenges for this instance.

"FILTERED you!" Holpa shouted.

The message disappeared.

Okay, I thought, that last one effected me directly. And it sucked, big time.

"It's okay," Shwenn said. "We can handle this. Not to worry."

"It's a live volcano!" Holpa said, looking exasperated.

Shwenn shook her head. "It's not an issue unless we let it be one. This doesn't change anything. We're still here and we're still going through with this. Besides, it's not like it can get any worse."

I spotted something flying through the air at us. "Look out!" I shouted and jumped.

The group barely had time to react as a red hot boulder plummeted from the sky and blasted the spot we'd been standing on. Sand exploded in every direction and the hot rock slid into the surf. Its near-molten surface caused the lagoon water's to hiss and steam.

Other rocks fell, splashing into the lagoon or raining down around the beach and jungle. For several moments smoking rocks and boulders pummeled the landscape while we alternated between dodging and cowering.

After several minutes passed, the nightmarish cascade of rocks ceased.

Dazed and bewildered I stood, looking around at the others as they recovered from the ordeal. "We okay? Everyone okay?"

Shwenn stood up, brushing sand off her robes. Despite this set back she still tried to remain positive. "We're good. It was just a show. It could have been worse."

Then I noticed the shattered remnants of Grumm's staff floating in the waves around the hissing boulder. A glance at my group bar showed his profile picture had been replaced by a skull and cross bones, and his hit points and mana bars were both at zero. He was dead.

Stunned, my eyes crawled down to the group combat log in the bottom corner of my vision.

Grumm Darkstone has suffered 7,680 hit points of crushing damage. Grumm Darkstone has died.

A cold realization hit me. Grumm was our main healer. *Had* been our main healer.

"No," I said, pointing at the boulder which had just crushed him to a pulp. "Things have gotten worse."

CHAPTER EIGHT

For several moments the group could only stare in disbelief at the hissing, steaming boulder in the surf.

"Okay," Witt said, "That isn't good."

Shwenn said, "This is just a set back. A big one, I know, but still only a set back."

"How can you say that?" Holpa said. "He was our healer."

"True," the fire mage conceded, "but we still have potions, and if needed, we could always retreat from a fight if we take too much damage and allow time to recuperate." She looked to Bozar and Holpa. "Both ogres and minotaurs have a racial benefit of health regeneration, so there's that."

"Mine's tiny," Holpa whined.

"That's what she said," Witt said with a grin.

The minotaur bristled, but didn't say anything.

Bozar nodded. "Yeah, we got regen, but it's like he said, it's almost inconsequential."

"Better than zero," Shwenn said, not wanting to let them wallow in the numbers. "Look, we'll fight smart. This doesn't change a thing. We still can make it through this instance if we don't let this set us back."

Another small boulder fell from the sky, but this one landed further down the beach, directly between the two statues. Apparently, it was enough to trigger the snakemen into action, as they suddenly came to life and looked around.

"Oh," I said, pointing. "Here it comes."

The snakemen turned in our direction, and in unison, slithered toward us up the beach.

You have been given a quest. 'Defeat the Coral Guardians'
Destroy the animated guardians to gain access to the rest of the island.

Reward: 1,500 experience points per group member.

"Okay, this is it, people!" Shwenn said.

Despite the morose attitude, everyone sprang into action, taking up their positions.

Shwenn summoned her pet, a diamond beetle the size of a desk. Large, scary pincer-like mandibles protruded from its head. She pointed at the fast approaching snakemen. "Sic 'em Charm!"

The beetle ran off, motoring down the beach kicking up sand as it went.

I positioned myself a few paces from Shwenn, placing myself between her and the jungle. That way, if it produced any surprises, she wouldn't be the first to get hit. I fired my bow at the snakemen as fast as I could. Bozar and Witt did the same although they missed more than they hit.

The two snakemen slid down the beach, jagged spears in their reptilian hands. As they got closer, I could see their light coloring was a mix of white and pink, and their flesh was pockmarked. Coral.

Charm the diamond beetle ran straight into one of the snakemen, causing it to stop and engage it. The coral guardian stabbed at the massive insect with its spear, but the beetle was quick, zipping forward and biting at its scaled belly.

The other snakemen didn't even turn to help its partner, instead, it came at the group.

As it got within range, both Bozar and Witt switched to their melee weapons. The ogre stepped forward first, getting the creature's attention. He held his huge kite shield high like a riot cop and swung out with his axe. Witt danced around the side of the monster and lunged when he could, hitting its side.

Shwenn produced a Wand of Energy Blast and pointed it. A small ball of static electricity zipped through the air to strike the snakeman on the chest. The damage it caused was small, but it didn't need her mana to be used.

Holpa stood a short distance on the being's other side and used a boomerang to attack, snatching the weapon out of the air as it returned.

For my part, I kept firing, knowing this was the most useful thing I could do at the moment.

The coral snakeman held its frightening spear in both hands and struck out at Bozar. The huge ogre barely came up to the thing's waist, yet he was still able to block its blows with his shield.

Witt danced back and forth, each time landing double strikes with his swords. He laughed. "Just keep chipping away at it! It's a one trick mob!"

As if the guardian understood what was said, it suddenly turned toward Witt and its long, muscular tail whipped around, slamming into the warrior's side.

Witt went flying several feet and landed in the sand, dazed.

Witt Middlehall has been concussed for 20 seconds.

"Oh, boy," I said, as I quickly switched to my sword and ran forward.

The snakemen returned its focus to Bozar with renewed vigor and one of its strikes glanced off his shield, lancing into his right shoulder.

With a grunt of pain, the ogre twisted back and slapped the spear away with his axe. His health bar had noticeably dropped.

As I reached where Witt lay prone in the sand, I activated my Shadow and charged around to the back of the snakeman. Its tail coiled behind it, kicking up waves of sand as it moved. With its attention on Bozar, I waited until it was the right moment and then slashed at it with my sword.

A large chunk of coral cracked off its body and the thing spun around with lightning speed to swing at me.

Thanks to my Acrobatics, I somersaulted over the spear and kicked off the base of its tail. It swung again just as I landed causing me to twist and jump backwards, but I wasn't fast enough. The tip of its jagged spear sliced across my stomach, drawing blood.

You have been hit for 185 hit points of slicing damage.

Bozar used this chance to hit the thing on its side, his huge axe breaking chunks of coral from its body. All the while this was happening, Shwenn kept up her energy assault. I knew what she was doing. She was the only remaining spell caster and conserving her mana for when it was really needed. Which might be soon.

Holpa continued to use the strange boomerang weapon, but I couldn't tell if it had any effect on the being at all.

As the snakeman turned to reengage with Bozar I glanced back down the beach at the other one.

Charm was doing a magnificent job of keeping the other snakeman in check. The diamond insect's hit points had been cut down to well below half, but the loyal pet wouldn't stop attacking.

Bozar managed a lucky strike and one of the snakeman's arms broke off at the elbow, and the being looked at the stump in confusion.

As if this were its cue, the other snakeman disengaged from Charm and slithered at us to join its companion. All the while, the beetle continued to bite into its whipping tail.

I turned to block the newcomer, knowing it could speed past and go for Shwenn. But as the thing barreled toward me, Witt ran in front and stopped its spear strike with crossed swords.

"I hate being concussed!" The warrior said as he exchanged blows. "I'm stuck watching my screen the whole time, and it drives me crazy!"

I glanced back at the first snakeman jabbing and slashing at Bozar. Holpa suddenly ran toward its rear, crystal dagger in hand and jumped over its swishing tail. He landed on its back, driving the crystal dagger into its coral flesh below the neck.

The being froze, as if surprised, and cracks spread from the dagger wound all across its body.

Bozar stepped forward and swung his axe, cutting through its midriff. The snakeman shattered into a thousand pieces, and Holpa jumped off.

The Coral Guardian has died. You have earned 400 shared experience points.

I whirled around to face the last one. Witt was doing a good job parrying the being's spear thrusts, but his shorter melee range kept him from getting close to strike. Charm had latched on to the base of the tale and was gnawing away, bits of coral spraying out the side of its mandibles like snow.

The full group placed themselves around the snakeman, with Bozar stepping in with his shield to relieve Witt, who was becoming exhausted.

"Ale!" Witt said, taking a few paces back to recover. "Gimme some ale and I could do this all day."

"You're out of stamina," Bozar said, bracing his shield against the blows. "Take a load off, I got this one."

I switched to my bow again and tried aiming for the thing's pitted eye sockets hoping to get an easy crit, but its movements were too erratic. As I changed target to its torso, Shwenn stood beside me.

"Okay, lemme try," she said, and cast Fireball.

Like a miniature sun, the lethal orb smashed into the guardian's chest causing it to rock back as if stunned.

Bozar leapt back away from the flames. "Oh, hey, watch that splash damage!"

"Sorry," Shween said. "Got carried away." She switched back to the energy wand to wait for her Fireball cooldown to reset.

Witt and Bozar continued to pummel the snakeman while the rest of us kept up the ranged assault. As we fought, I noticed a large crack had formed below its left collar bone.

Aiming for it, I used Sure Shot and fired.

The arrow lodged deep into the crack, almost disappearing. The next instant, the guardian seized up cracking all over, then it crumbled to the sand.

You have killed a Coral Guardian. You have gained 400 shared experience points.

"About time," Witt said dropping into a sitting position in the sand. "I hate statues. It's like their bodies are armor all the way through."

You have completed a quest: 'Defeat the Coral Guardians'.

The way into the jungle is now open for you to explore. Tread carefully.

Reward: 1,500 of shared experience points.

Shwenn looked around the group. "Okay, everyone is still alive."

"Except for our healer," Bozar said, quaffing a small healing potion.

"For this encounter," Shwenn said with a frown. She looked to me. "Are you okay, Viv?"

"Yup, just a scratch." The spear slice had dinged me pretty good, but I still had over a thousand hit points. I'd wait until it dropped more before committing to using one of my healing potions, of which I had six, as well as the three little health shots. I suspected the others were loaded up, especially the fighters, but didn't want to sound needy by asking them to share.

"Okay, loot time," Holpa said moving to the first corpse.

"Hey, knucklehead," Witt said. "Shwenn is group leader, so she doles out the loot."

The minotaur and warrior glared across the beach at each other. Holpa eventually looked away, snorting.

As Shwenn picked through the broken coral rubble of the first guardian's corpse, I angled myself so I could keep an eye on the beach, as well as the jungle treeline.

"Okay, gold first," the mage said, picking up a little money purse.

You have received 10 gold pieces of shared loot.

I smiled. Gold was good and this girl couldn't get enough of it.

"Two items," Shwenn said, picking one up. Its description appeared for all the group to see.

Item: Coral Ring of Water Breathing

Uses: 5 of 5

Durability: 40/40

Grants the wearer the ability to breathe underwater for a sixty-second duration.

Value: 120 gold pieces.

"Anyone need it?"

"Not even to swim out there," Bozar said pointing to the lagoon.

"Okay, dice it."

We all used the decision dice, 2D6, to see who won it and Holpa got the highest roll of eleven.

"Okay, next item," Shwenn said, holding up a helmet made entirely of sea shells.

Item: Charmed Helmet of the Ocean

Required Intelligence: 20

Durability: 35/35

Armor: 9

+25 Hit Points

+10 Mana

+1 Charisma

+2 Animal Charming (+5 for Sea Creatures)

Value: 1,850 Gold pieces

Everyone sat up straighter and grinned.

"That's more like it," I said. The gold value was good, but with the nice bonuses to Animal Charming ability, it would go for a lot more on the Marketplace.

No one could call need, because no one was a ranger by class, or an animal trainer by trade. So we went to the dice for it.

Shwenn won, and the others groaned playfully.

The next guardian corpse was a little more juicy in the loot department with three items.

You have received 12 gold pieces of shared loot.

Item: Coral Spear

Required Strength: 25

Durability: 26/32
Damage: 160-225
+15 Hit Points
+2 Constitution
+10% Spears
+5% Dodge
Value: 1,200 gold pieces

The dice gave it to Witt, who slid it into a Holding Bag. "This almost makes it worth getting knocked out for," he said. "Almost."

Item: Small Shield of Crushing
Required Strength: 20
Durability: 45/45
Block: +8
+25 Hit Points
+1 Constitution
+20% Clubs
+15% all Crushing damage
Value: 1,500 gold pieces

Shwenn arched a brow at Bozar. "This worth parting with that kite shield of yours?"

"Not even close," Bozar, said patting the image of his face on the huge shield. "This here is too uber to pass over for that trinket.

She looked to Witt.

"I'm a dual wielding kind of guy. Shields cramp my style," he said.

It went to the dice and this time I won with a nine of all things.

"Congratulations," Shwenn said handing it to me. Bozar and Witt offered me a slow golf clap.

There was no way I was going to use it so I managed to wedge the thing into my pack which took up nearly a third of its capacity.

The mage picked up the final item.

Item: Short Sword of the Wave
Required Strength: 20

Durability: 30/30
Damage: 45-60
+12% Swords
15% chance of casting Water Wave on hit.
Value: 175 gold pieces

The dice gave it to Witt who grimaced as he shoved it into his bag. "Borderline trash, there. But I'll keep it until something better needs to take its place."

Shwenn smiled as everyone gathered themselves and stood before her. "We did pretty good with that fight, especially Charm." She patted the diamond shell of the beetle at her side. "If we can keep this up, we should be able to clear out the island in no time."

I noticed Bozar and Witt exchange a glance. Holpa busied himself by kicking at the sand with a hoof. Maybe Shwenn could be a little too positive given the situation. If she noticed the doubt of the other members she didn't show it.

For me, based on how the group handled themselves I felt a little better about our chances, sans a healer. I even begun to think we could survive this.

But then Shwenn clapped her hands together and said, "Okay, lets go check out that giant shell over there. It looks so cute!"

Big mistake.

CHAPTER NINE

We stood around the stone platform on which the massive shell sat. No one wanted to commit to stepping onto it in case it was trapped.

Shwenn looked to Holpa. "Detect anything?"

Holpa rolled his eyes, but squatted down at the edge of the platform, examining it. I'd think that if he'd made it to level 50 as a minotaur, one of the first abilities he would've maxed out would be Detect Trap.

The minotaur moved around the platform checking as he went.

As he did so, I looked over the shell. It was a twisted version of a conch shell, with one end drastically tapered to a nozzle several feet above the ground. Its surface was a mix of opaque pink and white that swirled around its banded length.

When I queried the game as to what it was, it came up blank, like it was just a piece of uninteresting furniture. But it was far from that.

Holpa stood and shrugged his wide shoulders. "Looks clear to me, I think."

"You think?" Witt said.

"If there's a trap on there that I can't detect then it's a trap you want nothing to do with." The minotaur grinned and waved to the shell. "So why don't you go first?"

"Dice it," I said, wanting this little drama to end.

"Okay," Shwenn said.

I rolled a two.

Everyone laughed as I stood at the edge of the platform trying to scrutinize every detail. Finally, I shrugged and stepped onto it. Nothing happened.

Holpa said "That was anticlimactic."

"That's what she said," Writt said with a mischievous smile.

The huge conch gave no indication as to its purpose other than maybe it could be used as a horn. One end unfurled into a large opening, pointed at the sea.

"A warning horn?" Shwenn said.

I said, "Well, it's here for a reason. But if it's like everything else on this island, then it will probably try to kill us."

"Someone blow it," Bozar said.

"The shadow already lost that dice, she has to do it," Holpa said, with a sneer in my direction.

I shook my head. "Okay, unless someone votes no, I'm going to use it."

The others simply watched, curious.

"Fine," I said and pressed my lips to the little nozzle end. Inhaling deeply, I blew into it.

A loud blare boomed from the shell. The surrounding air shimmered with its intensity and leaves on the nearby trees shook.

Everyone clamped hands over their ears, cringing against the deafening sound. Even after I pulled away from the nozzle, the sound continued. Glancing at the lagoon I could see the sound creating little waves across the water and out toward the wall of storms.

For several long agonizing moments the sound shook the world and threatened to shatter my avatar's eardrums. Then, it stopped.

"Okay," Witt said, eyes wide and shaking his head. "Let's not do that again."

Shwenn frowned at the shell. "I don't get it. What purpose does this serve? Why have it here if it doesn't do anything?"

"It served to deafen us," Bozar said.

Holpa said, "Well, if there was anything on this island that wasn't aware of our presence before, they do now."

"I think people outside the instance could even hear that," Witt said.

Expecting something to come investigate the sound, the group angled themselves toward the jungle. But as I turned I caught movement out past the lagoon.

A swell of water was forming beyond the breakers. At first I feared a tidal wave, but the swell wasn't moving. Then I realized it. Something was rising.

"Guys!" I said, pointing out to sea. "I think we have another problem."

The swell continued to grow, like a large chunk of the sea floor was about to break the surface. Our ship looked small in comparison to it, pitching about riding the waves it created.

"I don't think this is going to be a good thing," Bozar said.

Whatever was below the surface began to move slowly toward the shore. It was huge. As it entered the lagoon, the clear waters allowed for a better look at what it was.

Long, thick tentacles. Huge globular eyes. A hood shaped head as big as the ship.

I recognized the creature, having encountered its Void cousins before.

"Leviathan," I whispered.

Someone gasped behind me, but I didn't turn to see who because the leviathan suddenly heaved up out of the water. Like a living mountain the monstrous creature continued to rise until the top of its long head reached past the tallest trees. Its mass of tentacles splayed before it, slowly probing about, exploring the lagoon's bottom.

But it appeared to have a destination in mind as it crossed the lagoon. The platform.

"I think we should run now," Holpa said.

"We can't be expected to fight that," Witt said. "How can we?" All his bravado evaporated at the sight of the monstrosity.

Shwenn stared at the leviathan with naked horror, her mouth working but without speaking.

"Shwenn," I said, moving close to gently nudge her. "I think this is one of those retreat scenarios."

The mage tore her gaze from the beast to look at me. "Yes. You're right. Everyone let us move into the jungle. If it gets up on shore, we can try and-."

The leviathan stopped, suddenly. The crest of waves it created surged up onto the beach, nearly reaching the platform. One of its house-sized eyes rotated to look at the ship, bobbing helplessly in the lagoon. Then the other eye did the same.

A tentacle emerged from the water and reached toward the ship.

"Uh oh," I said, fearing what was about to happen. "This will not end well."

The tentacle snaked over the bow of the ship. Then another tentacle joined it. Then more. Soon the leviathan turned, swelling the surrounding waters, and moved to the ship which looked half its size.

In moments, like watching a slow motion disaster unfold, the ship became ensnared in tentacles which covered the entire hull. The leviathan squeezed. From across the water the sound of cracking timber could be heard. With slow purpose, almost languid in motion, the leviathan grabbed the large center mast and yanked it. The great beam snapped like a dry twig, and it fell into the water.

Then the leviathan started to move again, its prey firmly in its death grasp. For a brief moment I feared it would continue its course to the platform where we watched in shock, but it moved out to sea past the breakers.

Slowly it began to submerge, huge founts of bubbling water geysering from beneath the ship and the monster's body. The last thing I could see of the creature was its eyes, staring in our direction as if to say it would be back. Then it was gone beneath the frothing waves.

For long moments, every member of the group was silent, too stunned to say anything.

Then Witt said, "I think I just FILTERED myself."

I said, "I believe we've just proven that blowing the horn was a bad idea."

The lagoon's water swirled and heaved in the wake of what had happened, looking empty without the ship.

Shwenn ran a hand down her face and sighed. "Okay, this is a set back."

"Ya think?" Said Holpa, who looked the most upset out of all of us. "Now we're really trapped! How do we get back to the FILTERED gate?"

"Something will present itself," Shwenn said, looking for a silver lining. "There has to be another way off. We just need to find it."

Bozar held up a Teleport Token in his thick fingers. "These are completely useless, too. After all that gold buying it, and it's worthless here."

I said, "That thing had to be a part of a bigger story, here. You don't randomly place a leviathan, of all things, in an instance without a good reason."

"Like what?" Asked Witt.

"Maybe we were never meant to take the ship back to the gate," I said. "That leviathan was simply an event the game created to ensure that. I think Shwenn is right, there's another way off this island, maybe another ship, or a gate, or something. And we have to find it."

Trying to raise everyone's spirits, Shwenn clapped her hands together. "Okay, people. Look alive. This isn't the end, this is only the beginning. We have no other choice but to continue on. Bozar, would you be so kind as to lead the way?"

Leaving the shell-horn behind, we turned and followed the path into the jungle. In moments, the lagoon vanished from view as we were swallowed up by the thick vegetation.

Bozar took front with Witt a few paces behind. I kept beside Shwenn, feeling protective of her. Mages were not known for their high hit points and heavy armor. Behind us trailed Holpa, who's head snapped around at any sound.

Having the huge thief at my back made me nervous, and I kept checking on him as much as the jungle we traveled through.

As we moved along, I spotted a bright blue flower in the tall grass. On impulse, I picked it.

You have acquired an item: Sky Flower

The petals of this flower can be used in various potions.

Value: 3 Gold Pieces

Herbology Skill Increased! Level 1, 26%

"I've never seen that before," Shwenn said to me.

"What," I said. "A leviathan?"

"Yeah, heard about them. Seen vids of other guilds being wiped by them, but not one so close. Have you?"

An image of the Kraken pulling itself through the Void portal and into Ogden's lair flashed in my mind. "Nope," I said. "Never."

She shook her head slowly. "Just when you think this game has thrown everything at you something like that happens."

She was silent for a few moments, then said, "I love this game."

"Me, too!" I said, and we laughed.

"Shh!" Bozar said, suddenly stopping. "There's something ahead, on the side of the path."

From our vantage point, it looked like a small structure was sitting squat in the thick grass. Most of it was masked by trees.

"Let me check," I said, then dipped into Shadow form.

As the others waited, I moved forward along the path, my eyes on the strange structure. As I got closer its details became more clear.

Keeping my distance I walked past the screening trees and stopped, surprised.

A small airship lay in ruins in the vegetation, its massive balloon deflated and covering a wide area like a rotted whale carcass. The structure seen from the path was its travel basket which lay on its side.

Unlike the airships used for transport, which were as big as sea-bound vessels, this one was tiny in comparison. At best it could carry three or four passengers, of which there was no sign.

I looked into the basket and found no one there, except riggings and empty cases. Then something caught my eye on its exterior. An arrow. I plucked it out and examined it to find it was normal, save for red feathering and a barbed head.

Slowly, I turned around, taking it all in. There was nothing else about, so I dropped out of Shadow and waved to the others. "All clear."

As they approached, they took in the scene.

"Oh, wow," Witt said. "Someone crashed here?"

"Looks like," I said, looking over the surface of the huge deflated balloon.

Holpa's eyes lit up, looking genuinely excited. "This is how we get out of this place! We use this airship to get back."

I shook my head, "Not going to happen unless you have some made airship-crafting skills." I pointed at the massive tears in the balloon. "Looks like the trees really did a number on this, ripped it to shreds."

Shwenn said, "Any idea how long ago this happened?"

"No idea," I said.

A message appeared.

You have found a quest. 'What goes up, must come down.'
Find out what happened to the survivors of the airship crash.
Reward: 500 shared experience points.

"Well, there is our rescue mission," Witt said with a chuckle. "Never enough of those around."

"I think we're the ones in need of rescuing," I said.

"Shh! Listen!" Bozar said, suddenly raising his axe for quiet.

A deep base thumping could be heard from somewhere within the jungle ahead. It was a constant beat, like a section of music that played over and over.

Drums.

I held up the red fletched arrow in my hand. "My guess is natives."

"At least it's not snakes," Holpa said, looking nervously at the trees.

"They probably took the survivors," Shwenn said listening to the drums and scanning the jungle. "I think it's coming from that direction. They obviously know we're here so let's head over to them."

Suddenly, from the vegetation she pointed at, burst forth several little men wearing snake masks. They were almost completely naked save for a type of bamboo armor which covered their bodies. Each were armed, some with primitive axes and bamboo shields, or bows nocked with red fletched arrows.

Their skin was covered in a light green paint, fading to white in some areas. But upon closer inspection I realized that it wasn't paint, but scales. And their faces weren't masks at all, they were truly reptilian in appearance.

"Or they could come to us," Shwenn said taking a step back.

The natives formed a row before us, about a dozen in all.

My group quickly positioned themselves as best we could, with Shwenn at the rear.

For several moments, neither side moved, sizing each other up.

Witt was coiled to strike, rocking back and forth on his heels, twin swords at the ready. "These pipsqueaks don't look so tough."

"Don't jinx us," I said.

Suddenly, from the depths of the jungle, the drums went silent. The natives froze as if surprised, then they raised their weapons and shields above their heads and shouted a word over and over.

"Sisoria! Sisoria! Sisoria!"

Then they attacked.

CHAPTER TEN

As the natives rushed forward, Bozar shouted out his War Howl.

The effect was immediate as nearly all of them surged at the ogre. He buttoned up behind his massive shield, swinging his axe in wide arcs.

Witt attacked the scrum from the edges, striking a native from behind. The native turned to hack at him with an axe.

Holpa backstabbed one attacking Bozar, then turned to parry a swing from another with his short sword.

This left three natives with bows standing back and firing arrows. Dipping into Shadow, I zigzagged at them. The jungle shadows kept my ability maxed to the point I was nearly invisible, even while sprinting.

Shwenn sent Charm into the throng around Bozar, then fired her energy wand. These natives had high hit points, and could take a lot of damage.

Running up beside one of the archer natives, I blinked out of Shadow and struck him from the side. He dropped his bow and pulled out a small axe, lunging for me. I back-pedaled while parrying his strikes. The strength behind his swings was a little scary, but I kept from getting hit.

The two other archers were entirely focused on Bozar, and hitting him with each shot. The ogre's hit points were dropping at an alarming speed.

Shwenn cursed, and fired a Fireball at the two archers, who didn't even bother to move out of the way. The Fireball exploded around them, sending them flying into the vegetation. Bushes and branches caught on fire.

A Sisorian Native has been killed. You have gained 600 shared experience points.

A Sisorian Native has been killed. You have gained 600 shared experience points.

The native hacking at me with his axe glared and hissed. He looked human, but his skin was entirely of little scales, and the eyes in his human face were long narrow slits. A forked tongue flickered out of his mouth.

I kept smacking away each of his attacks, but he wouldn't let up. Without thinking, I parried a swing then lunged forward in an attempt to run him through. But he easily dodged to the side and swung downwards, hitting me in the back with the axe.

Cursing, I pulled away. That hurt. These guys had some serious punch.

Over the native's shoulder I could see Bozar was swinging like a maniac, but strangely, none of the natives were dead.

Witt faced off against three natives who had broken away from the Bozar dog-pile. With dual blades he matched their attacks swing for swing, but I could tell he was a little concerned with their fighting abilities.

Holpa, for his part, was jumping onto the backs of natives and jamming his crystal dagger into them. But when he pulled away, he was surprised to see they didn't drop dead.

"What's up with these guys?" I shouted to Shwenn as I parried another brutal axe strike.

"I think they have an insane regen ability," Shwenn said, focused on her wand attacks.

Great, I thought and tried for another lunge. This time, I hit home, drawing blood. But the native barely flinched still swinging like crazy.

Okay, this wasn't working. To Shwenn I said, "Get Charm onto this guy, and hit him with your wand."

Perhaps realizing what I was doing, she did so without argument. The diamond beetle pulled away from gnawing on the leg of a native to race across the grass. It rammed into the back of the native I was duelling with and clamped its pincers onto his leg.

The native turned to look, almost as if annoyed. At the same moment, an energy ball from Shwenn's wand struck him in the face.

While he was distracted, I stepped forward and jammed my sword into the center of his chest. The blade went right through his odd bamboo armor and out his back.

He hissed in pain and glared at me with red-slitted eyes. But he didn't go down. As I slid my blade out of him, he resumed his attack, but this time his strikes were much weaker.

But after exchanging several blows he suddenly buckled and fell to one knee. Charm suddenly snapped its pincers around the side of his head and squeezed. The native hissed in pain, and I ran him through with my sword again. Finally, he crumpled to the jungle floor.

You have killed a Sisorian Native. You have gained 600 shared experience points.

I ran to where Witt was fighting the three natives, barely keeping them at bay. Charm drove into the legs of one, and I hacked at the native's exposed back. As he turned in surprise, an energy ball struck his head.

I hacked and sliced at his torso while he parried some of the strikes. These guys were tough.

To my right, I was aware that Bozar had killed one of the natives and managed to quaff a healing potion. All the while the others continued to strike at his shield or hit him with their axes.

Witt suddenly took a nasty hit to the face while parrying a blow and stumbled back. His health bar took a big dip. A crit.

"FILTERED!" Witt said, shaking his head. "Can we set this to easy mode now? These dudes are hardcore!"

The native I was tangling with hacked at my sword as I continued to parry them.

Parry Skill Increased! Level 6, 59%.

Charm was practically eating through his leg, but he didn't seem to mind. The leg should have been ripped off by now. If these natives had a regen ability, it was off the charts.

Then, as the native tried to push me backwards with a flurry of attacks, his red eyes widened. I noticed a black swirling cloud dance across their surface and then was gone.

Uh oh.

"Dark magic!" I shouted for all to hear. "They're under the influence of Dark magic!"

Even over the sounds of combat I heard several filtered curses from the other members. Dark magic perverted normal magic like a radioactive bomb. The Dark magic no doubt strengthened these guys and enhanced their natural regen ability, but at the cost of something else.

Shwenn cursed. "Okay. Not good."

But there was little to do about it right then except to fight for our lives.

Suddenly, Charm bit through the leg of the native and he collapsed, a surprised expression on his face. I took the chance to drive my sword right through one of his slitted eyes, piercing the brain and getting a fatal crit. The native's body sagged.

You have killed a Sisorian Native. You have gained 600 shared experience points.

With the native dead I quickly looked to Bozar who I was concerned about as he was taking a serious beating. Despite having just taken a potion, his health bar was back down to half again as the natives didn't let up their attack.

Holpa focused his attacks on the same native Bozar was and managed to backstab the reptilian man. The being shrieked and collapsed to the ground.

A Sisorian Native has been killed. You have gained 600 shared experience points.

Witt and Shwenn focused on one of his two attackers in an effort to chip away at its health together, with Charm doing its leg attack thing.

Wanting to help Bozar, I quickly ran a few paces back from the fray and switched to my bow.

Aiming at the native Bozar was exchanging blows with I fired a Multi-Shot. Instantly, four arrows sprouted from the native's neck and he arched his back in agony. Under continual barrage, Bozar lunged forward with a concentrated swing and his axe cut the native's head off.

Now there was four natives on Bozar and two on Witt.

Having to wait two and a half minutes for my Multi-Shot cooldown to reset, I took aim at the head of one Witt was trying to wear down. I fired a Sure-Shot into the being's head and it died on the spot. That was it for my bow abilities for the moment.

I gave Bozar a glance, and he nodded. Certain he was okay for the moment I fired a rapid series of volleys into the final native on Witt. Within moments, the native's back was a pincushion of a dozen arrows. With Charm sawing away, Witt's counter strikes and Shwenn's energy blasts, the native finally succumbed.

You have killed a Sisorian Native. You have gained 600 shared experience points.

"We having fun, yet?" Witt said as he charged over to help Bozar. With a running leap he drove his twin swords into the back of a native. Amazingly, the native turned to hit Witt across the face with its axe.

"FILTERing Dark magic FILTERED!" Witt shouted as he recoiled from the blow. "Shouldn't even be in the game! Makes everything over-powered!" He parried a series of axe blows.

"You'll get no argument from me," Shwenn said firing her wand. "No wonder this instance has such a low success rate."

Bozar swung out with his axe, hitting two of the natives, before ducking behind his shield again. "What is it?"

"Twelve percent," Shwenn said.

"Well," Witt said, "I don't intend on being a part of the eighty-eight percent. We're twelve percenters, right guys?"

Everyone was too busy fighting to answer. The way things were going, we might not make it into the twelve percent club at all.

I kept to my bow shot, knowing I could do the most damage this way while being more selective of my target. A quick volley on the native Witt had engaged helped turn the tide, and the snake-being dropped.

You have killed a Sisorian Native. You have gained 600 shared experience points.

After taking a deep cut to his side, Holpa backed away from the fight and took to using his boomerang again. I couldn't blame him. As a thief, he shouldn't even be on the front line, but there was little choice in the matter.

There were three natives left, and we kept the group's entire focus on one of them at a time. With Bozar absorbing their strikes and quaffing potions, he held their attention enough for us to whittle their hit points down to zero. One by one they fell, until all three were dead, giving me an additional 1,800 shared experience points.

When the last native had collapsed, the group sighed with exasperation.

"What a grind," Bozar said, sagging against a tree. "That Dark magic stuff gives them a heck of an advantage."

Witt said, "If the rest of this instance is like that, we're going to be at this for a while. Regardless of what I hit those guys with, they just wouldn't go down."

I asked Shwenn, "What's the most effective thing against a Dark Magic attack?"

"Dispel Magic," she said. "Which I have."

"Great!" Witt said.

"And it has a one hour cooldown," Shwenn said.

"Which is not so great," I said with a wry grin.

Witt noticed Holpa snooping through the native corpses. "Hey, FILTERED! What did I tell you about the loot procedure?"

Holpa rolled his eyes and went to crouch under a tree. The thief looked beat up, and I was actually a little impressed he had held his own. Despite all his whining he could still put up a good fight.

Shwenn quaffed a mana potion, then went to the corpses.

"No, take a break Shwenn," Witt said. "You've earned it."

"It's okay," Shwenn said. "I wanna see what these guys got."

First, she went to each corpse to check for gold, netting each of us 210 gold pieces. I smiled as the coins clinked into my money purse.

Then she went through the items. Not all the natives dropped something, but there was a good number to go around.

These three items went to Bozar.

Broadsword of Destruction
Required Strength: 35
Required Agility: 22
Durability: 35/35
Damage: 245-285
+10% Swords
+15% Double Handed Weapons
+1 Deadly Strike
+3 Path of Destruction
Value: 3,500 Gold Pieces
Bamboo Chest Plate of Sisoria
Required Strength: 32
Durability: 45/45
Armor: 28
+15% Heavy Armor
+20% Poison Resistance
+10% Dark Magic
+80% Hit Points when in the presence of Sisoria
Value: 2,800 Gold Pieces

Axe of Silence
Required Strength: 28
Required Agility: 25
Durability: 30/30
Damage: 145-190
+15% Axes
+5% Dodge
30% Chance cast Silence spellcasters on hit.
Value: 1,400 Gold Pieces

These two items were won by Witt.

Dagger of Wounds
Required Agility: 30
Durability: 32/32
Damage: 125-150
+15 Damage
+20% Daggers
45% chance to cause Bleeding Wound on hit.
Value: 1,300 Gold Pieces

Boots of the Jungle
Required Strength: 20
Required Agility: 22
Durability: 30/30
Armor: 12
+15% Light Armor
+30% Sneak when in jungle terrain.
Value: 700 Gold Pieces.

This item went as need to Holpa.

Bracer of Secrets
Required Agility: 25
Durability: 35/35
Armor: 10
+15% Detect Traps

+10% Detect Treasure
+5% Find Path
Value: 2,600 Gold Pieces
This went as need to Shwenn.
Ring of Mana
Required Intelligence: 30
Durability: 40/40
+130 Mana
+8% Mana
+5% Mana Regeneration
Value: 1,650 Gold Pieces
And I got this which I immediately wore.
Amulet of Power
Required Level: 45
Durability: 35/35
+25 Hit Points
+2% Hit Point Regeneration
+10% All Damage
Value: 3,500 Gold Pieces.

"That was an okay haul," Bozar said, his eyes on the jungle. "But I would have expected more considering how tough those mobs were."

"Preaching to the choir," Witt said.

Shwenn said, "Gentleman, loot isn't just given away. It must be earned. And, as usual, it's never good enough. Ever."

We moved past the corpses to stand on the path. The jungle revealed nothing of what lay ahead.

"Maybe it will get easier from here on out," I said, teasingly.

"Don't jinx us!" Witt said as the group continued on.

Turns out, I did.

CHAPTER ELEVEN

We cautiously moved along the pathway, all the while watching the dense vegetation for signs of an ambush.

Everyone was on edge after the fight. The strength and resilience of the natives made each one of the group uneasy, particularly Witt.

He said, "Shwenn, if Dispel magic negates Dark magic, why didn't you cast it back there? We could have used the help."

Shwenn frowned, not keen with the implication she didn't know what she was doing. "The spell doesn't work like that."

"Then how?" Witt said.

The mage took a breath, and I could tell she was trying not to lose her patience. "Casting it on one of them would have only done some damage to the Dark magic in their bodies. Sure, I might've been able to kill one, but with the one hour cooldown on the spell, I needed to save it."

"For what?" Witt said, getting annoyed. "Until one of us gets killed?"

I found myself ticked off with his attitude and answered for Shwenn. "She needs to save it in case one of us gets hit with Dark magic. That's more important."

Shwenn nodded. "That's true. If one of us gets hit with Dark magic, I need to Dispel its effects quickly. Most Dark magic spells are damage over time, or binding. Without my Dispel, you'd have to wait for the Dark magic to dissipate, if it does at all."

"Okay, fair point," Witt said, calming down. "Didn't mean to snap at you, Shwenn."

"It's alright," Shwenn said. "We're all a little frazzled after that encounter. It was tough, but we pulled through it."

Bozar said, "Now I can see why so few people make it through this place. This instance doesn't pull any punches. Reminds me of the ones you can find deep in the Ice Fields of Yindle. Those are so tough, you have to give up and label them as RR."

"What's RR?" Holpa asked, clutching the boomerang in one hand, and his short sword in the other.

"Reroll," Bozar said. "As in that's the end result if you were dumb enough to go inside. This Emerald Caldera is like that, an RR instance. I'm beginning to think we made a mistake coming in here."

To hear Bozar say so was telling.

"Great," Holpa said. "We're in a guaranteed reroll instance without a means of escape or Teleport Tokens." He shook his head.

Shwenn said, "We all knew this was a possibility when we signed up. Not like it's coming as a sudden revelation. Besides, knowing that certain death could lurk just around the corner makes the game more fun."

Oddly, I found myself thinking about how I didn't want to leave this terrible place. The Shadow Blade was here, somewhere. I didn't care about the Caldera's quests or even about the group at all. They were all a means to an end. One that would get me another Legendary item.

Playing in these MMOs can make one pretty cold, almost mercenary in the approach to others in the game. I used Shwenn to get a spot on the group, and she used me to gain access to the instance. And now that we were here, beyond that little arrangement, I didn't care. I wasn't vested in the experience, or crossing it off my list of instances to conquer. I was here for one loot item only.

Witt was about to say something else when Bozar raised his axe, stopping the group.

Ahead were some ruins. A wall of old stone, choked with vines and covered in vegetation, crossed our way. The path led to a narrow gap between its stacked stones.

After a moment, Bozar signaled for us to continue. At the wall, he poked his head through the gap, seeing if it was clear. Satisfied, he nodded and walked on to the other side. We followed.

Beyond were more ruins. Ancient buildings surrounded us, forming a long courtyard. Every stone or brick was cracked and eroded with age. Vines and vegetation covered everything, so much so it was hard to tell if it was buildings we were looking at or hilly mounds.

Several doorways and windows dotted the structures, but no light came from inside. Looking closer at the exposed stone showed carved reliefs of snakes coiled around people, or swallowing them alive.

Midway down the courtyard Bozar stopped and glanced at Shwenn. "What should we do, boss? Investigate?"

The mage surveyed the buildings, trying to decide.

Holpa said, "I think we should just log out now, while we still can."

Shwenn looked at him, incredulous. "And then what? What could that possibly serve?"

Holpa said, "Then we pay for a Location Transfer from customer support. Get them to move us back to Helto Port."

Witt scoffed and Bozar groaned.

Shwenn shook her head and glared at the giant thief. "You don't play the game just to pay for a Location Transfer whenever you want. That's cowardly."

"No it's not," Holpa said, getting defensive. "It's smart. If it keeps you from having to reroll and level all over again, I don't see anything wrong with it."

I asked, "Have you ever paid for a Location Transfer before?"

The minotaur glanced at the others sheepishly, then said, "Yeah."

"How many times?" I said.

"A bunch," Holpa said. Seeing our disgust he quickly added, "It isn't that bad. All those times it was life or death, you know. And I don't have the time to retread old levels."

I said, "That's part of the spirit of the game. The fact you can die at any moment and have to start all over again. That's part of why we're all here now, the thrill of a potential permadeath. Paying for a Location Transfer just because you can't use a Teleport Token goes against that."

The Location Transferring service provided by UFW was controversial for as long as it had been available. Nearly thirty years prior, they introduced the service in a bid to get more money from their playbase. And people happily paid for the exact reasons Holpa said. But for the vast majority of players, it was plain wrong and ruined the experience for those who knew the risks they took in game.

Witt shook his head. "Man, that's weak. Do you plan on using a location service to get out here, now?"

"Maybe" Holpa said, almost petulant.

"And what about us?" Bozar said, his voice rising.

Holpa shrugged. "If you were smart, you'd do it to."

"You'd abandon us here?" Witt said.

The minotaur shrugged. "It's not like you really need me." He pointed at me. "You already got a thief."

Everyone groaned and shook their heads.

But before anyone could verbally lambaste Holpa for his admitted cowardice, someone called out.

"Beg pardon, but might I interrupt?"

Caught off guard, the group whirled around in the direction of the voice, weapons at the ready.

Standing in an entrance to one of the ruined buildings was a man. Tall and lanky, he wore simple clothing as if he were out on a stroll, rather than in a lethal island-jungle. Dark boots came up to his knees, and a wide-brimmed hat did little to contain the tangle of gray hair beneath it. On his nose perched a pair of spectacles with one lens cracked.

He looked at our stunned expressions, then said, "Sorry to be a bother, but might you consider keeping it down? There are natives everywhere and you're only drawing attention to yourselves, and, in turn, my hiding spot."

I was the first to get over my surprise and said, "Who are you?"

"Me?" He said, a little annoyed by the question. "I'm the man telling you that making loud noises in this place is most certainly not wise if you wish to stay alive. But if you insist on speaking then perhaps you can do it inside here." He pointed back to the room behind him.

I looked to Shwenn, who shrugged. "Well, we would like to speak with you," I said.

The man nodded, "Then come in, and do it quickly please, they may come by at any moment."

Shwenn said, "Okay, let's check this out. Be on your guard."

Bozar was the first to follow the tall man back through the entrance. Looking around, he turned to us and gave the all clear.

Carefully, we filed inside to find ourselves in a large, low ceiling chamber. The far side had crumbled into ruins with a gap between the stone blocks that led to a dark hall. Two windows allowed for a view of the courtyard outside.

The tall man looked us over and nodded. "So, you're on an expedition, too, I take it?"

"In a manner of speaking," I said. "We're adventurers on a hunt for treasure."

The tall man let out a tittering sound and I realized it was laughter. He said, "Oh, well you will certainly find treasure here. But whether you survive to leave with it is another matter."

Getting back to my original question, I said, "Who are you and what are you doing here?"

"Oh, where are my manners," the man said, extending a hand. "My name is Nigel Bridgestone of Bridgestone Explorations. And you are?"

"Vivian Valesh," I said shaking his hand. I introduced the others in turn and Nigel insisted on shaking their hands, too.

"A pleasure to meet you all," he said. "Certainly nice to encounter someone from civilization. As to why I'm here, well my company had sent me looking for the Emerald Caldera in hopes of making contact with the lost tribe of Sisorians. Turns out, we found both, unfortunately."

"That's your airship, out there?" I said.

"Correct. It was my airship, but now is a complete wreck." His face suddenly brightened at a thought. "Might you have a ship, here? I'm in need of transport and am willing to arrange payment once we make it to the nearest port."

"No," I said. "Sorry, we don't. Not any longer."

"Oh, dear," Nigel said. "Then it appears I'm stuck here for the duration." He gave the ruined chamber a mournful look.

Quest competed. 'What goes up, must come down.'

You have located one of the survivors of the airship crash. Find out what he knows about the island.

Reward: 500 share experience points.

Shwenn asked, "What happened to your airship?"

Nigel said, "Oh, after leaving Grishen City we sailed in the direction we thought the island might be hidden. After several days, we drifted right into the worst storm you could imagine. Tossed us about like a fly in a kettle. Fortunately, it spit us out right over this island, and the moment I saw it I knew this was the Emerald Caldera. But the damage from the storm was too great, and we crashed into the jungle. Not long after, the Sisorians arrived and took my assistant and the airship captain. I managed to escape unnoticed and found this place. A dreadful episode, all together, if you ask me."

I said, "How long have you been here?"

"Six days and five uncomfortable nights. But I haven't been sitting in here waiting to die. I'm an explorer after all, so I've been venturing into the jungle looking for things to eat and such."

"So, your assistant and the airship captain have been kidnapped, and need rescuing?" I asked, waiting for the quest to appear.

"No, they don't need rescuing anymore, as they are dead."

That explained the lack of a rescue quest. "What happened to them?"

"They were fed to the great Sisoria over at the main temple. Grisly affair that."

Bozar asked, "How do you know?"

"Because I saw it! Like I said, I've been exploring about, looking for food, and eventually I happened upon the massive ruin complex at the base of the mountain. Well, volcano, now. Anyway, hiding up in the jungle I was able to see down into the complex which is shaped like a bowl. At the bottom rests the great Sisoria who guards an ancient tomb."

You have found a quest. 'Enter the tomb.'
Kill, or evade Sisoria to enter the ancient tomb.
Reward: 1,500 shared experience points.

"Who is this Sisoria? One of the natives?" I asked.

"No, not at all. See, I'd been doing research on the myth of this place and wanted to find it myself. Legend says that the natives here found a huge conch by the lagoon one day and decided to sound its horn."

"Sounds familiar," I said with a frown.

"This summoned Sisoria from the great depths of the ocean to this island. Here, she used her Dark magic to transform the human natives into a reptilian mutation who, for generations, live and die to serve her every whim."

"Why would you even want to come to this place?" Holpa said, incredulous.

"For science, my good man!" Nigel said, offended. "Why do it for any other reason? Why did you come here?"

"Loot," I said.

"Oh," Nigel said, "that's a good reason, too, I suppose."

Shwenn asked, "So this Sisoria guards a tomb?"

"Correct," Nigel said. "I've seen it from outside, at the mountain, er, volcano. She coils herself outside its entrance and never leaves it unguarded."

"Coils?" Holpa said. "What do you mean by coils?"

"As in a snake, my bullheaded friend. Sisoria is a serpent of great size and power."

"Snake," Holpa said, his voice trailing off in disbelief.

"Wait," I said, "so the natives blew the horn and accidentally summoned her here. But we just blew the horn, too."

"And?"

"And bad things happened," Witt said, with a frown.

"A leviathan appeared and destroyed our ship," I said.

Nigel looked aghast. "Really? Why that's most incredible. I would have thought the horn was only meant to call Sisoria, but it appears that theory is no longer valid. Perhaps it calls whatever leviathan is nearby, and Sisoria happened to be closest when the natives used the horn."

Shwenn asked, "What about this tomb? Is there treasure inside?"

The explorer shrugged. "I could only guess as I didn't have the nerve to sneak around Sisoria to look. It is certainly a possibility as there are several legends that indicate so. Some say she brought the treasures up from her lair at the bottom of the sea in her stomach and regurgitated them into the tomb. Another legend says the treasure was already there when she arrived and claimed it as her own. But whatever is in there, you can be certain it would be important."

Like a Legendary blade, perhaps? I thought to myself. "Where is this tomb?"

Nigel pointed northward, "Not too far from here. The island isn't that big so you really don't have to go far to get anywhere. Especially if you are looking to die."

"Why do you say that?" Bozar said.

"Because Sisoria has hundreds of natives at her disposal. They guard every inch of this island. And, I'm not sure if you're aware, they are very tough to kill."

"Hundreds of them?" Holpa said, mortified.

"Yes," Nigel said. "Like a little army. Perhaps she someday plans to leave this place and conquer one of the larger nearby islands. Who's to know."

"I don't like this," Holpa suddenly blurted. "This isn't what I signed up for."

"What the heck are you talking about?" Witt said, rounding on the minotaur.

Holpa shook his head. "I'm all for a tough adventure, but now we have to face a giant serpent-leviathan thing as well as hundreds of those little FILTEREDs? We barely survived a dozen, how are we going to take on hundreds?"

"It's all part of the game, Holpa," Shwenn said. "The challenge is half the fun."

Holpa laughed. "Half of your fun, maybe, but not mine." He marched back into a dark corner of the ruins. Finding a little alcove he crouched inside.

"What are you doing?" Shwenn said, alarmed.

"I'm logging out," Holpa said. "And, yes, I've paid for location transfers before and I'm going to do it this time as well. This place is a guaranteed RR, so why not? It's not like I'm going to miss out on anything."

Witt roared and suddenly ran at Holpa, swords drawn. But Shwenn stood in his way.

"Don't!" She said. "If this is what he wants, then fine."

Holpa's eyes glazed over and his body went still. A clock appeared above his head, counting down from five minutes. Once the five minutes was up, his avatar would be removed from the game.

"That son of a FILTERED!" Witt said. "I knew he was going to pull something like this."

Shwenn tried to calm the warrior down. "It's okay. We'll be okay. We don't need him. Whatever this game throws at us, we'll handle it without him."

Somewhere in the distance the drums started up again, this time louder and more frenetic.

"Incoming!" Bozar said, standing next to the entrance. He looked outside with worry.

Through the windows I could see dozens and dozens of natives suddenly pouring into the ruined courtyard. In moments, several hundred assembled themselves outside. Each one was facing the chamber we were in.

"Oh, dear," Nigel said, staring at the army outside. "This is most unfortunate."

Looking at the mass of tough mobs, I had only one thought.

Guess it was time for a reroll.

CHAPTER TWELVE

I moved up to one of the windows, bow in hand.

The sight of all the reptilian natives was both shocking and awe-inspiring. This time, there were more varieties of weapons being wielded by them; spears, nets, tridents and the jaw-bones from large, toothy creatures.

But one native stood out above the rest. He wore a large plumage headdress and held a snake-shaped scepter which had a head of a cobra.

"A witchdoctor," Nigel said from beside me. His eyes were wide with terror. "He'll have Dark magic spells."

"Form up!" Shwenn shouted. "Bozar, block the main door, Witt take the window opening on the other side." Bozar was already in place and Witt quickly moved over to his position. Shwenn stood behind Bozar with a view out all the openings.

I said to Nigel, "You might want to fall back a bit in case they start firing arrows."

Nigel nodded and retreated to the darkened gap at the back of the chamber.

"Hey, does that go anywhere?" I said to him, pointing at the gap.

"I don't know," Nigel said. "I've only gone in so far to, uh, relieve myself. I don't have any light orbs. It might."

I looked to Shwenn. "That's our fall-back position." We would need it.

The throng of natives hadn't made any move toward the chamber. Instead, they simply stood outside and waited patiently. The drums continued, getting faster and faster.

"Should I start shooting?" I asked, uncertain. "They're going to hit us soon, anyway."

As if in answer, the drums stopped. The natives outside all raised their hands and together chanted, "Sisoria! Sisoria! Sisoria!"

"Oh, how interesting," said Nigel, curious despite himself.

I glanced back at Holpa's avatar where it still stood in the shadows, timer ticking down. Part of me wanted to run him through, just for kicks. He'd left us at the worst time, but the selfish part of me understood him to a degree.

A cheer from the mass outside pulled me back into the situation.

Dozens of native archers fired their bows in unison.

"Duck!" Shwenn said.

I didn't need encouragement and dropped below the window ledge just as a torrent of arrows blew through it and into the chamber. I glanced over at the others.

Bozar hide behind his massive kite shield, its edge flush with the stone floor. Arrows ricocheted off of its hard surface, the *thunking* of the impacts sounding like rain.

Both Shwenn and Witt moved to the sides of the other window, waiting for the assault to peter out.

Witt caught my eye and shouted, "We having fun yet?"

The arrows stopped, and I dipped into Shadow to peek outside. My eyes barely made it over the window's edge when my view was blocked by natives running toward me.

"Here they come!" I shouted and popped out. I immediately used my Multi-shot in an arc, hitting four at the same time. It didn't even slow them down as they reached the window in a run. Taking a quick step back I headshot the first one with my Sure-Shot, and he stumbled backward.

As the three front-runners reached the window, I switched to my sword and attacked like a madwoman. I knew my attacks could only whittle away their health, not kill them outright.

Bozar braced his kite shield from the attacks by leaning his body against it. From over its top he swung his axe, trying for exposed heads.

Witt was slashing wildly, hacking away at the natives trying to climb through. Shwenn was at his shoulder, zapping away with her wand while Charm snapped its pincers onto anything that crossed the threshold of the sill.

I knew in that moment that we weren't going to make it. Not even close. The natives were too strong and in such great numbers holding them back, let alone defeating them, was impossible.

But I fought on regardless. Hacking at limbs that over extended, or jabbing at reptilian faces which hissed at me.

Suddenly, something brushed past my leg and Charm motored up to the window to clamp onto an axe wielding arm.

"Thought you could use a little reinforcement!" Shwenn said with a grin as she turned back to her window.

And I did. The natives were pushing harder to get in, but the small openings of the windows worked in our favor. Bozar's shield nearly blocked the entire entry way like a reinforced door, but the natives were pounding on it with incredible power.

A Sisorian Native has been killed. You have gained 600 shared experience points.

"The first of many!" Witt shouted, pushing the limp body of a native back out the window. The fact that it had taken so long just to kill one was depressing, but I'd take it for now.

A heavily injured native at my window was trying desperately to squeeze past the others to get inside. With all my strength, I lunged forward and plunged my sword through his hissing face until it came out the back of his skull.

You have killed a Sisorian Native. You have gained 600 shared experience points.

Swords Skill Increased! Level 9, 74%.

"See, first time wasn't a fluke!" Witt shouted, hacking and slashing.

I shouted to Shwenn, "Fireball time?"

"Saving it for if we fall back!" She said.

If we fall back? I thought. It was guaranteed to happen.

One of Bozar's axe swings finally cleaved a head.

A Sisorian Native has been killed. You have gained 600 shared experience points.

Then, another message followed.

You have increased a level! You are now 47! Congratulations! Earned: 3 Attribute points, 5 Skill points, and 3 Ability points.

Great, I thought. Now if I could just live long enough to distribute them, I'd be happy.

We all knew that this was a no win situation, but none of us would say it. Doing so would mean admitting that Holpa was right on some level. Yes, it was hopeless, but no, we weren't going to be cowards about it.

As Charm bit down on an arm, the native it belonged to fell back, pulling the large insect along with him. In an instant the diamond beetle vanished into the throng and was set upon by dozens of weapons.

Shwenn gasped as Charm's health bar was pummeled to zero. Her pet was dead.

This shifted the tide. The natives at my window pushed harder to get in, and despite my best efforts, I could barely keep them out. A glance toward the others told me the same situation was happening to the whole group.

"Prepare to fall back!" Shwenn shouted, reaching into her robes. She pulled out a handful of small orbs which she then tossed into the air. They flew along the low ceiling until one hung above each person's head, then light up. Light orbs.

I glanced back at Nigel who was peering back into the tunnel with the light of his orb. "How's it look, Nigel?"

Nigel jumped at my shout. "Oh, it's a long tunnel, but I can't see far. It looks to head deeper into the complex."

That's all I needed to hear. We had an out, for however long it lasted.

Suddenly, the natives at the window stopped attacking and stepped back. In fact, all the others did the same.

In unison, the natives walked backwards, never taking their slitted eyes off us. After a dozen paces they stopped, forming a living wall. Behind them, over a hundred others waited.

I switched to my bow and nocked an arrow.

"Hold it!" Shwenn said. "Maybe they want to talk."

Talk? I thought. This was a prelude to disaster as far as I was concerned. But I held my shot for the moment.

The drums started up again, and the natives resumed their chant.

"This can't be a good thing," Witt said.

The natives parted and the witchdoctor stepped forward. He held the snake scepter high and glared at us. It was obvious he was going to cast something nasty.

"Shwenn!" I said.

"Got it," she said and stepped forward. Sticking her hand outside the window she cast her Fireball.

The molten orb slammed into the witchdoctor, engulfing him in flames. He fell to the ground, dropping the scepter.

I tensed up, drawing my bow.

But no one attacked to avenge their fallen leader if that's what he was. Instead, all the natives continued to stare at us, chanting incessantly.

Then it occurred to me. "No death message," I said.

Shwenn cursed.

The witchdoctor slowly stood, flames engulfing his headpiece and flesh. While still ablaze, he knelt down and picked up the scepter.

I'd seen enough. "Screw it," I said and fired a Multi-shot at him.

But the arrows barely crossed over the windowsill when the witchdoctor quickly pointed the scepter in my direction. The arrows dissolved in mid-air.

From behind us, Nigel said, "Perhaps we should run now?"

Faced with an unkillable Dark magic spellcaster, Shwenn made the call. "Okay, fall back!"

Nigel backpedaled as I followed Shwenn into the gap. A glance told me it was a narrow tunnel made from the same blocks as the rest of the ruins. Where it went was anyone's guess, just as long as it got us out of there.

Witt backed up to the tunnel's entryway. Bozar still blocked the door with his shield in case they suddenly rushed. I could see over his shield at the witchdoctor, skin on fire, pointing his scepter again.

"Bozar! Run!"

The ogre started to step back toward us, still braced against his shield.

From the witchdoctor's scepter a black shadowy smoke shot forward. The smoke quickly enveloped Bozar who looked at it in confusion. The smoke solidified, turning into a large black snake. The creature became solid already coiled around the Slayer and squeezed. All of this happened in the span of a second.

Bozar gasped, dropping his axe, his shield wedged up against him within the snake's coils.

"Bozar!" Witt said moving to help him.

The witchdoctor snapped back the scepter like a fisherman pulling on his line. The next instant, Bozar was yanked out the door and vanished into the crowd where he was set upon.

Shwenn grabbed at Witt's shoulder. "No! He's gone! We have to go, now!"

As if to reinforce her statement, the natives ran forward in unison, all the while chanting.

I grabbed at Shwenn. "Go! Lead the way!"

She only hesitated a moment then rushed down the tunnel.

Witt was ready for a war having just stood by helplessly as his friend was taken. To rub salt in the wound, Bozar's health bar was beat down to zero until his profile picture was replaced by a skull and crossbones.

"FILTERED!" Witt said.

I pulled at his arm as natives spilled through the door and windows. "Back up, now!"

Despite his rage, he had the presence of mind to retreat into the tunnel staying close to my shoulder.

I, too, backed up, but didn't run. Instead, I withdrew my one and only Disorientation arrow and nocked it.

The natives were jostling and knocking each other over in their need to get to us, which worked in my favor. The more in the chamber before I fired, the more of an obstacle they would create for the others.

Waiting until the last possible moment, I fired up at the center of the low ceiling. The chamber exploded into an array of bright lights. Multi-colored strobes danced around the space, blinding everyone inside.

The effect was immediate. The clamoring throng turned into a mosh pit of blind natives blocking the entrance and windows. But it wouldn't last for long.

I turned and gave Witt a shove. He was itching to jump in and strike while they were helpless, but there were a lot more outside waiting to rush in. This was our only chance to get some distance.

The warrior cursed and turned to follow the others. Trailing behind him, I kept firing into the chamber, every shot hitting. I did that the entire length of the tunnel until it suddenly turned.

Then I followed the others into the darkness of the temple ruins.

CHAPTER THIRTEEN

The tunnel continued straight after the first turn and gradually descended. The walls tapered upward forming a narrow triangle, and we passed several carved reliefs all depicting snakes devouring people.

"Do you know how far this goes?" Shwenn asked Nigel.

"I can only guess, miss," Nigel said. "But one could assume that it connects to the main complex to the north." The explorer kept stopping to examine the glyphs and reliefs. Witt would grumble and give the awkward man a gentle shove.

"We got nasties on our tail, buddy," the warrior said. "No time for sight seeing."

Only a few minutes had passed since we escaped from the chamber. The effects of the Disorientation arrow would have expired by now and, no doubt, our pursuers were trying to catch up.

My gaze went to the group list at the side of my vision and I suddenly laughed. "Check out Holpa's health bar."

The thief's hit points had been cut in half and dropping fast. In seconds, they hit zero and a skull and crossbones replaced his minotaur's face.

Witt and Shwenn laughed and gave each other a high-five.

"Serves that FILTERED right!" Witt said, keeping Nigel moving along. "Looks like he got that transfer he wanted, but straight to the newbie zone."

The natives had made short work of his idle avatar, but were they still interested in us? The acoustics in the tunnel were warped, and the sounds of our footfalls and breathing masked any signs of pursuit.

We moved quickly through the darkness, Shwenn's light orbs barely revealing what was a few steps ahead.

I was still a little in shock over Bozar's fate. It happened too quick with no way to help him. Just like that, a tough, geared up level 52 Slayer had been essentially nuked out of existence.

"I can't see how this is a six-person instance," I said, constantly checking behind us. "What sort of groups have survived this craziness?"

"Tough ones," Shwenn said, peering ahead as we moved. "My guess is they didn't have the restrictions we got stuck with."

"Or lost their healer the moment they landed on the beach," Witt said. "This would be a totally different situation if Grumm were still with us. We might have even been able to mulch through that lot back there."

"Something is ahead," Shwenn said. Several dozen paces further down, the tunnel ended in a t-junction. From the left turn came a bright red glow.

"Lemme take point, Shwenn," Witt said, moving up front. We followed him as he carefully approached the junction. He glanced around the corner in both directions, and his shoulders sagged. "Well, this makes our choice easier."

The left tunnel had collapsed a dozen paces down, cut in half by a hissing stream of lava which bubbled out of a crack in the wall.

To the right was more tunnel.

As we turned to go down Nigel stopped. "Wait," he said. "I think this direction is a bad idea. The main temple structure is that way."

"So?" I said, keeping a nervous eye on our flank. There was still no signs of pursuit, but it didn't mean they weren't coming.

"Sisoria is there!," Nigel said, eyes wide. "If we encounter her, then that would be the end of us."

"It's not like we can go back the way we came," Witt said. He pointed a thumb at the lava. "And that way ain't an option either."

As they spoke my eyes fell on a cluster of yellow lichen which grew in a stone crack. On impulse, I picked a wad of it off.

You have taken an item: Deep Earth Lichen This lichen can be used in various high level potions and salves.

Value: 2 Gold Pieces.

Herbology Skill Increased! Level 1, 27%.

Nigel still looked nervous. "I'm at a loss as to what to do. Maybe the natives have left and we can go back?"

I knew he was speaking out of fear. He wasn't an armed adventurer like the rest of us. "We're here for the treasure, which means the tomb is our destination. You can come with us, or stay here. Up to you."

I didn't intend to sound mean about it, but it was true. His options were limited.

Nigel blinked his eyes and looked at us a little sheepishly. "Yes. Yes, of course. Foolish of me to suggest otherwise. I wasn't thinking. It's just that I've never found myself in such a life or death situation before."

"It will be a death situation if we don't start moving again," Witt said, nudging the man forward. "So let's keep putting those feet one in front of the other."

With no other choice, we continued down the tunnel which leveled out. In a few minutes it ended at a small alcove. A large, featureless door was set into the opposite wall.

Shwenn stopped at the edge of the alcove, her light orb floating forward to illuminate it better. "Careful, might be traps here." She pointed at two elevated stones in the middle of the floor.

"If it's a trap, then it's being a little too obvious," I said, peering inside.

The door was blank, with no hint as to how to open it. The tapered walls extended high above forming the alcove into a hollow pyramid. No reliefs or glyphs adorned the walls.

Witt crouched down, examining the floor. "Can't believe I'm saying this but we could really use Holpa right now." He turned to me. "You're a thief, aren't ya? Don't you have Detect Trap?"

"Not anymore," I said, shaking my head. "Once I switched to Shadow at level 20, I paid a heap of gold to redistribute my points into the abilities best suited for my subclass. Sorry."

Shwenn looked to Nigel. "Any ideas what this is?"

Nigel shrugged his bony shoulders. "None, other than to step on one of those stones and see what happens."

Suddenly, there was a loud cracking sound from behind. A section of the wall a dozen paces down collapsed inward and a stream of lava spilled forth into the hall.

"Okay," Witt said. "We need to hurry this up!"

"Wait," I said. "Everyone back up a bit from the alcove."

We shuffled down tunnel as far as we dared, all eyes on the growing flow of lava. Aiming at the left stone with my bow, I fired.

The arrow bounced off its surface, but the stone didn't move and nothing exploded. I did it again with the other stone and got the same results.

"We should throw something heavier at it," Shwenn said, casting furtive glances at the advancing lava.

"Okay, who wants to part with some loot?" I said.

"Not me!" Witt said with a grin. Even in the face of certain death his greed won over.

Nigel said, "Here, try this." He reached into the satchel at his hip and pulled out large bunch of bananas. "I was going to save it for later, but I think they would make a worthy sacrifice to the cause."

I took the bananas, hoping they would be heavy enough. Carefully, I walked to the edge of the alcove and threw them the short distance to the stone.

The bananas landed, and the stone sunk down, stopping flush with the floor. Somewhere over the bubbling and hissing of the lava, came the sound of a loud click.

"Okay," I said, looking to Nigel. "Got anything else?"

He dug around for a few moments then produced a large coconut. "Will this do?"

I laughed and took it. "Got a turkey dinner stuffed in there, too?"

"Well, you never know when you're going to get hungry," he said.

"Any time, guys!" Shwenn said. A short distance behind, a section of the hallway's ceiling fell into the lava.

I threw the coconut onto the other stone which pressed down as well, followed by another click. But nothing happened.

We looked around in confusion, and Nigel said, "It's obvious both stones cannot be pressed at the same time. Might I suggest removing the bananas as a test."

I reached out with my bow and used it to snag the bananas. Even as I did it, I could feel the growing heat of the molten pool behind us. Quickly, I yanked them off the stone. The stone depressed to its original position, and another click sounded. This time, the stone door opened, slowly retracting into the ceiling.

I nocked a bow and Witt stood beside me, swords at the ready. But the new entrance only revealed the tunnel continuing on.

Carefully, I stepped over the stone plates and checked the doorway for anything dangerous. Satisfied, I stepped through. I didn't die.

"Okay, let's keep going! Quickly!," Witt said.

As the others passed through the alcove, Nigel said, "Can I have my coconut back?"

"Not this time, buddy," Witt said.

Once on the other side we paused, and I said, "Should I knock that coconut off and see if it closes the doorway?"

Witt looked to me and said, "Do it."

I shot at the coconut shattering it with my arrow. The stone depressed and the door slowly ground down to a close. I noticed Nigel giving the door a plaintive look. "This is a one way trip for all of us," I said.

We continued on, following the new tunnel which looked identical to the ones before it.

As we hustled along, Shwenn suddenly cursed.

"What is it?" I asked.

"I'm multitasking here," she said. "I got a notification that Holpa, or rather the player behind him, has filed a complaint against me and Witt."

"What the FILTERED for?" Witt asked.

She said, "He's claiming we bullied him into entering an instance we knew to be RR, and then forced him to log off in a dangerous area. Because of that, he says we got his avatar killed. He's seeking an Administrator to step in and restore his character."

"What a FILTERED!" Witt shouted. He went off for several moments with a stream of filtered words.

Shwenn said, "He's also asking that we have our accounts reviewed and we're either banned outright or heavily penalized. The rat is also demanding his share of any loot we get."

Keeping my eyes ahead on the hallway, I said, "It won't happen. I've never heard of such a thing going too far past an Administrator." The game company received complaints similar to this all the time. Usually, it came from spiteful players looking to cause grief to others.

"We should file a complaint against him!" Witt said.

"For what? Being a coward?" I said.

Witt said, "For abandoning us like he did. There's got to be something in the Player Code of Ethics, right?"

"Hate to say it," I said, "but that's even weaker than Holpa's case. Who reads the PCE anyway?"

Witt knew I was right and launched into another filtered tirade.

Throughout all this, Nigel was silent, as if the conversation didn't even register with him. As an NPC he wouldn't be expected to comment, or even recognize, real life related talk between players.

As if to remind us where we were, the tunnel suddenly ended at a large rectangular chamber. We carefully entered, watching for raised stone plates on the floor.

The light orbs showed another tunnel on the other end, from which a faint light could be seen.

Shwenn waved her hand for everyone to be quiet. "We'll talk about this later."

"That's guaranteed," Witt said.

Cautiously, we crossed down the length of the room to the other tunnel entrance. Dipping into Shadow, I peeked around its corner. The tunnel extended away about two dozen paces to a brightly lit exit leading outside.

"This is it," I told the others.

We moved toward the exit, mindful of our steps. I was in front with Witt directly behind me, followed by Nigel and Shwenn.

Through the exit, I could see a rocky slope far across an open space, a trickling of lava cascading down its surface. Telling the others to wait, I tiptoed forward until I was at the edge of the tunnel.

Outside, was a large sunken colosseum, shaped like a bowl as Nigel had described. Comprised of concentric levels of cut stone, it was the size of a sports stadium. Other tunnel entrances dotted the ruins, of which many were expelling lava.

Directly across was the mountainside. Its shattered peak vomited massive plumes of smoke high into the sky. Huge rivers of lava gushed forth and down its rocky face, threatening the ruined colosseum.

All this was a lot to take in, but what was at the very bottom of the huge, open air structure got my full attention.

There was an entrance leading into a portion of the ruins set into the mountain, the same triangular shape of the tunnels.

In front of the entrance, resting peacefully in a massive coiled pile was the single largest snake I had every seen. It was so long and large, it rivaled the grav-trains of Mars which raced between its domed cities.

I was even more awestruck at the sight of the creature than I had been with the leviathan. They were of equal titanic proportions. This was the god the natives worshiped and I could see why. The thing demanded respect and fear and got both in equal measure from all who gazed at her.

Sisoria.

CHAPTER FOURTEEN

I stepped into the tunnel and walked back to the others, dropping my Shadow.

Seeing my expression, Shwenn asked, "What is it?"

"We're doomed," I said.

"Why?" Shwenn said.

"Take a look for yourself," I said, motioning to the exit.

Witt and Shwenn moved to look outside while Nigel trailed behind.

"I've seen her before," Nigel said. "I don't need to do so again, if you don't mind."

"I don't blame you," I said, and went to stand behind the other two.

Witt was beside himself. "That's guarding the FILTEREDing entrance? It's a monster!"

"Keep your voice down," Shwenn whispered. "We don't know if it can hear us up here. But you're right, she's a monster."

We stared at the gargantuan creature at the bottom of the ruined colosseum. Simply looking at it one could tell it was worthy of a much bigger group, like an army.

"I don't think we're meant to kill it," I said.

Witt looked at me, hopeful. "What do you mean?"

"Look at the quest to enter the temple," I said. "It specifically says to sneak past or kill her. Gaining entrance doesn't mean we have to fight, not that we could."

Shwenn reread the quest text and smiled. "Oh, I like that." She looked down at the slumbering beast. "Well, Viv, I think this is something you could do in your sleep, but what about us?"

"Yeah," Witt said. "What about us? My sneaking skill is like level 1 at four percent and the last time I used it was back in the newbie zone."

"Same here," Shwenn said. She looked to me. "Any suggestions?"

There was a part of me that wanted them to just go away. I could sneak in there myself and retrieve the Shadow Blade, but I had no idea what I may encounter. I doubted it would be something a solo player could handle alone. If there was a chance for me to get the Blade, I'd need these two just in case.

I looked at Sisoria and the ruined tiers that led down to her. The entrance to the tomb was not on the same level as her, but the next one above. Getting these two down there would be a heck of a task.

I pointed at the tomb's entrance. "See how the entrance is not right at the bottom? That means we don't have to cross paths with her at all. If we stay quiet and move slowly down, tier by tier, we should make it."

Sisoria's head was pointed southward, more or less in our direction. "Let's move around to the other side of her before moving down."

"Why?" Witt asked.

"Because if she opens her eyes, we'll be behind her. And if she does, freeze. I think it would reduce our chance of being detected." Or so I hoped. Honestly, I had no idea if that was true, but it sounded good and it made the others a little more confident in what amounted to a suicide attempt.

Shwenn nodded, staring at the huge serpent. "Okay, sounds like a plan. Why don't you lead the way, Shadow?"

Nigel cleared his throat. "If you don't mind, I will remain here until you return. Climbing about anywhere near that devil will make me lose my nerve. I've seen what she can do and the furthest away I can't get, the happier I'll be."

I looked to Shwenn and Witt who both shrugged. "Okay," I said to Nigel. "Stay out of sight and whatever you do, don't make a sound."

Nigel said, "That will not be an issue in the slightest, my dear. I've learned the art of being inconspicuous over the last several days."

As Nigel retreated into the tunnel, I surveyed the colosseum. Following the tier to the right meant crossing over some gaps and rubble, but would take us all the way to the other side behind the serpent.

The left was cutoff halfway around by several streams of lava which formed spattering waterfalls of death down each tier. The right side it was, then.

To the other two I said, "Stay low and against the wall along the tier. When we reach an obstacle watch how I cross and do the same. Once we're on the other side, we'll help each other down. And if that thing opens its eyes, or moves, make yourself as small as possible and hold still."

"And if it sees us?" Witt said. Despite being a tough player and a fierce warrior, he looked genuinely worried.

"Then we die," I said. "Come on."

As we moved along the tier I stayed out of Shadow so they could see me better. I judged the distance to the other end to be roughly two hundred paces away. My entire focus was to get there as quickly as possible.

I glanced back at the others who were close behind, first Shwenn, then Witt. Their eyes were wide with apprehension. Good. It meant they'd be more careful, or so I hoped.

We slinked along, mindful of wide cracks and loose rocks. About forty paces along was a jagged rock pile of stone which had slide down from the tier above. It looked recent, probably caused by the volcano's eruption.

Taking a quick scan I chose the least cluttered spot, one with fewer exposed stones. I slowly climbed, placing one foot at a time so the others could see what to do. At the top of the pile I perched and watched as they followed. Shwenn appeared to have a higher climbing skill than Witt and easily traced my foot placements. Witt, with his bulkier armor and impatience, grew frustrated almost immediately.

Catching his eye I motioned for him to slow down and take it easy. The proud warrior grunted, but did as I indicated.

Before Shwenn reached the top, I started down the other side. Suddenly, a small slab of stone cracked beneath my weight and crumpled further into the pile.

Everyone froze, our eyes going to the sleeping serpent below. The creature hadn't moved, nor did its eyes open. I gave it to the count of five before continuing down, this time testing the stones before committing my full weight.

Reaching bottom, I stood back to watch the others. They were exceptionally cautious for which I was appreciative. Once they both stood before me, we continued on.

The next fifty paces went smoothly and put us directly at the halfway point. A large crack blocked the way and was about five paces across. For anyone with even a moderate Agility it wouldn't present a problem, like myself. But I wasn't sure about the others.

I motioned them into a huddle, and as we crouched down together I spoke in a hushed whisper. "Any problems for you guys with this jump?"

Witt shook his head. "Not a problem. I only need a small run at it and I can clear it."

I looked down at his heavy boots which had thick soles. "Take those off first, and make sure there's nothing loose on your body that could make noise as you run, or land."

Witt looked a little surprised by this, then shrugged and yanked off his boots.

To Shwenn, I asked, "And you? Can you make it?"

The mage looked genuinely bashful at the question. "I've been sinking every spare Ability and Skill point into anything but whatever it would take for me to make that jump. So, no. I don't think so."

I nodded, expecting as much. "No worries, we'll get you across."

Witt handed me his boots then took a few steps back. After a few seconds of psyching himself up, he ran. At the edge he jumped and vaulted across the open space without issue. But as he landed, he stumbled and ducked into a roll along the ground. The pommels of the twin swords on his back clanked loudly against the stone. Coming to a stop, his head snapped in the direction of the snake. So did mine.

Sisoria was awake.

I caught my breath and heard Shwenn do the same. Instinctively, I went into Shadow, knowing that one less intruder to potentially detect might help.

I prayed to the Gaming Gods for the coiled terror to close its eyes. If it did, I promised to always be a good Shadow, and never do anything bad again.

The Gods were not listening.

The huge snake lifted its head and turned in our direction. A forked tongue flickered from its mouth, testing the air. For several moments its slitted eyes remained locked on us.

There was no way of telling if it could actually see us, or was simply looking in the direction the sound came from. But it didn't matter as she started to move and slithered toward us.

Shoot, I thought, looking for a way out of this. The only option I could think of was to run back to the tunnel entrance, but that only contained a terrified explorer and a literal dead end.

Suddenly, Witt stood, shouting and waving his arms.

I wanted to ask what the heck he thought he was doing, but it was obvious. He was acting as a distraction.

"Hey, over here FILTERED! Come give daddy a kiss!" He shouted. Without looking in our direction he said, "Get into that tomb and loot the FILTERED out of it. I'll see how long I can keep this FILTERED entertained." Even before he finished speaking he pulled himself over the edge of the tier and dropped to the next one down.

Shwenn grabbed my arm, eyes wide in shock.

The serpent was now moving quickly, first arching its head up over the first tier, then sliding up onto the next. Her eyes were locked on the crazy warrior making a scene.

At the other tier, Witt turned back in the direction we'd come, then ran and jumped over the crack again. Landing on the other side, he ran as fast as his socked feet would let him.

Sisoria was in full hunter mode and turned away from us to give pursuit. She was four tiers below Witt and moving like a grav-train at full speed.

Watching the insane drama unfold before me, I had the presence of mind to shake my head. To Shwenn I said, "We go! Now!"

The mage blinked away her shock then nodded. "What do we do?"

I motioned for her to get up on my back, which she did after a moments hesitation. Then, holding onto her legs with her arms around my neck, I ran at the crack. At its edge I jumped using my Leap ability. Without it, the extra weight would have pulled us short. Instead, we landed on the other side with a grunt from Shwenn.

As she slid off my back we both looked to the other end of the colosseum.

Witt was tearing along at a great speed, but the serpent was much faster. The snake was nearly even with the fleeing warrior and quickly moved up two tiers, closing the distance between them.

I pulled at Shwenn's arm. "Come on!"

Fully intent on taking advantage of this opportunity, we ran down to the end of the tier. Then I dropped down to the next level and motioned for Shwenn to do the same.

She looked at the drop and blanched. "I can't!"

"Yes you can, I'll catch you."

Grimacing, she spun around and hung over the edge by her hands, then dropped. True to my word I caught her by the waist and kept her on her feet.

Sisoria moved up to the same tier as Witt and was sliding up behind him like a missile. The warrior was still shouting, like it still mattered. But just as the snake was about to catch up to him, he reached a tunnel entrance and bolted inside.

The snake didn't even slow down before she plowed her head into the narrower space. She didn't slide in, but she wouldn't give up. Her momentum and colossal size imploded the stone around the tunnel entrance as she struggled to get in. Her body wiggled and thrashed about, kicking up rocks and crushing the ruins beneath it.

Aware we were running out of time, we dropped down two more times until we reached the bottom tier with the tomb.

We ran to the entrance, and I used my Shadow to peek inside. It was a long vaulted tunnel the same shape and size of the entrance and vanished from sight.

The sound of screaming made us look back. Incredibly, Sisoria had pushed herself into the tunnel nearly half her immense length. I couldn't tell if the sound I heard was actually screams from Witt or noise from all the carnage the serpent wrought.

Shwenn and I stared at the thrashing tail of the serpent as it slowly disappeared into the tunnel.

I gave the mage a nudge, then together we reluctantly turned away and went inside.

CHAPTER FIFTEEN

We moved through the huge entryway tunnel keeping close to the walls. The sounds of the ruins crumbling outside soon faded as we got deeper.

Quest complete. 'Enter the tomb'
Reward: 1,500 experience points

Shwenn called up her light orbs again, illuminating an architecture identical to what we'd encountered before. The only difference was the size of it.

"This is Sisoria-sized," I said, realizing what it meant.

"What?"

"The tunnel. Its design so she can come in and out without a problem."

Shwenn didn't look thrilled by this bit of information. "Maybe she'll get stuck back there and we won't have to worry about her again."

"They come back," I said. "Monsters always do."

The tunnel continued straight into the base of the mountain and I was very aware lava was potentially flowing just beyond the walls. If the lava got behind us, we'd be in big trouble.

"Hey," Shwenn said. "I need a little break, please. This has gotten me all hot and sweaty in my simulation suit. I need to give it a little time to air itself out."

"Okay," I said. As much as we needed to be moving, I could understand. My simulation suit was also having trouble keeping up with drying my sweat away. This game made for a heck of a workout sometimes.

We crouched in a small alcove. I kept looking back toward the entrance, but didn't see any movement. I wondered how Witt was doing and checked his party profile. His health was at full, so there was that.

"He's not dead," I said. "Guess he's good at running."

"He's got the motivation to get better at it," Shwenn said, and we laughed a little. "He may be able to avoid Sisoria, but I don't think he'd last long against another group of natives."

"There weren't any natives in the colosseum back there, not that I'm complaining," I said. "My guess is they're out looking for us."

We were quiet for a few minutes, then Swhenn asked, "Hey, can I see your Cloak's stats? I've always been curious."

I wasn't surprised she knew about my Cloak. Most people did by now as Legendary items were hard to keep a secret. I suspected that was part of the reason she took me up on my offer to get the statue from Xorrox in the first place.

"Sure," I said. "Lay your eyes on this."

Cloak Of Shadows (Legendary)
(Shadow Class Only)
(Level 40 required)
(Agility 45 required)
Bonuses:
+100 Hit Points
+5 Constitution
+1 Dodge Skill Level
Abilities:
Summon Shadow Steed (Mount)
Teleportation (Level 1)
Invisibility (Level 1)
Phase (Level 1)
Void Portal (Level 1)
Shadow Master, Legendary Set Pieces: (1/4)
Cloak of Shadows (set bonus +1 Sneak Skill Level)
Shadow Blade (set bonus - unknown)

Boots of Shadow (set bonus - unknown)
Shadow Guard (set bonus - unknown)
Full Set bonus - unknown

Shwenn's eyes widened. "Impressive. And it's part of a set, too. Good luck finding the others."

I wanted to say one of them was right here on the island, and most likely within this very tomb. Instead, I said, "You never know when you might come upon one in this game, now that they're everywhere."

"Not quite everywhere," Shwenn said. "I don't have one."

Fight a god, I thought. "Maybe that can be your next quest chain to chase after."

A crumbling noise a short distance ahead made us jump to our feet, weapons at the ready. Keeping Shwenn behind me, we waited.

Several moments passed and the crumbling sound came again, this time closer.

"What is it?" Shwenn said, wand held in front of her.

"Sounds like something in the walls up ahead on that side."

"Lava?"

"Dunno, but we need to move."

We headed down the tunnel, keeping to the opposite wall from where the crumbling came from. As we passed by, the wall behind us suddenly collapsed inward, revealing another smaller tunnel.

"A secret tunnel?" Shwenn said, peering into its darkness.

"It's not a secret anymore," I said, then jumped back as something emerged from the tunnel's blackness.

A large snake slithered forward and entered the main hallway. Shwenn and I backed up, ready for this new threat.

This snake was nowhere near the size of Sisoria, but it was big enough to be a problem.

"May I?" Shwenn said as the snake reared its head up. It towered over us both.

"Be my guest."

The mage cast her Fireball, and it shot across the hall at the snake. The flaming orb exploded against its raised neck and the creature hissed in pain, collapsing to the floor.

Quickly, I ran over and hacked at it with my sword. The thing snapped at me and I rolled out of the way, just in time.

Dodge Skill Increased! Level 7, 13%

Coming out of the roll, I swung around to strike its flaming flesh. The creature rolled away, twisting and contorting in agony.

Stepping back, I switched to my bow and fired several shots into its head.

You have killed a Giant Viper. You have gained 400 shared experience points.

Next to its body appeared two small gems, one red, the other blue. I picked them up.

You have acquired an item: Small Opal
Value: 250 Gold Pieces.
You have acquired an item: Small Ruby
Value: 250 Gold Pieces.

I held them out to Shwenn in my hand. "Go ahead, pick a color."

She crooked a brow in contemplation. "I always liked blue, so I take that one."

Tucking our loot away, I gave the new tunnel a look. It appeared to go on for a dozen paces or so, but beyond that was darkness.

"We can check this out on the way back. For now, let's keep going, okay?" I said.

"Sounds good to me," Shwenn said.

We followed the tunnel until it suddenly ended at a massive chamber. It was shaped like a hollowed out pyramid with its upper reaches hidden in darkness. There weren't any entrances or doors along its walls. At its center was a raised dais on which a large golden chest sat.

Shwenn whistled at my side. "This looks like the place."

"Yeah, but what surprises might it have?" I picked up a couple of rocks and rolled one along the floor until it bounced off the edge of the dais.

"Wait here," I said.

"If you insist," Shwenn said with an impish grin.

Frowning, but sword at the ready, I stepped into the huge chamber. Carefully, I padded across the floor until I reached the chest. I glanced up and was struck with a sense of vertigo looking at the empty void above me. Shaking my head, I examined the chest closer.

It looked like a fairly standard issue chest, like a trunk. There didn't appear to be any clamps or locks on it. As for traps that was anyone's guess.

"It's safe up to here," I said.

Shwenn walked over, her eyes drinking in the sight of the chest. "Oh, I wonder what's inside!"

"Should I open it?"

"Are you sure it's not trapped?"

"Not at all."

"Then, please, be my guest," she said with a laugh.

Carefully, I opened the chest.

Inside was a heap of gold coins and items. Although not even close to the size of Xorrox's treasure, it was enough to make me smile.

I waved at the loot. "Why don't you do the honors again."

"Are you sure?"

"Why break with tradition?"

Shwenn stepped up to the chest and ran her hands through its gold which vanished.

You have received 955,256 Gold Pieces.

I whistled. It had been a while since I was flush with cash and this put me back on top, again.

She took each item out one at a time.

Item: Staff of Resistance

Required Level: 45
Durability: 35/35
Damage: 125-155
+85 Mana
+15% Resist Magic
+15% Resist Disease
+15% Resist Cold
+10% Resist Fire
+25% Resist Poison
Value: 2,500 Gold Pieces
This one I let Shwenn have as it was something she could use.
Item: Ring of Freefall
Durability: 45/45
+3 Freefall
Value: 850 Gold Pieces
We diced for it and I won.
Item: Crown of Thorns
Required Level: 42
Durability: 40/40
+10 Armor
+20 Hit Points
Damage 25-35 to attacker when wearer is hit.
Value: 1,200 Gold Pieces
We diced and Shwenn won.
Item: Breastplate of Defense
Required Level: 44
Required Strength: 45
Required Agility: 35
Durability: 60/60
+25 Armor
+145 Hit Points
+1 Level to Dodge

+1 Level to Parry

Value: 5,200 Gold Pieces.

Shwenn won the dice on that one.

Item: Boots of Sneaking

Thief Only

Required Level: 45

Required Agility: 42

+8 Armor

+25 Hit Points

+1 Level to Sneak.

100% Silence when walking.

Value: 8,200 Gold Pieces

Although I insisted on dice, Shwenn gave this to me outright, which I immediately wore.

Item: Broadsword of Anguish

Required Level: 42

Required Strength: 50

Required Agility: 35

Durability: 50/50

Damage: 225-345

+45 Damage

+5% Chance of Paralyzing opponent on hit for 20 seconds.

+55 Hit Points

+1 Level to Swords

Value: 10,600 Gold Pieces

We diced and Shwenn won again.

The final item was interesting.

Item: Gem Box of Many

Required Level: 40

Durability: 45/45

When placed inside, will change a gem into another random variety of equal value and size. Cooldown 2 minutes.

Value: 15,000 Gold Pieces

Even at such a high value, this item could go for ten times that at the Marketplace. The box was a must-have for Jewelers.

Drooling, we diced, and I won.

Satisfied, we stashed our loot items away in our packs.

"So, was this worth it?" I asked.

"It never really is, is it?" Shwenn said. "I mean, when can you say you've ever been completely satisfied with a loot drop at the end of an instance?"

But before I could answer, Shwenn suddenly looked over my shoulder and froze, eyes widening in fear.

I instantly recognized that look and spun around, sword at the ready.

A dark shape was moving down the tunnel from the distant entrance. For a few moments I could only stare, knowing what was coming. My eyes went to the party profiles at the edge of my vision and saw that Witt was dead. It must have just happened.

"She got Witt," Shwenn said, seeing the same. She stood beside me, wand in hand. "We need to be running now."

I shook my head. "Run where? She's blocking the only way out."

"What about that side tunnel?"

"Right."

Then we were moving, racing down the tunnel toward the fast approaching serpent.

As we ran, I could see the broken wall with the tunnel entrance up ahead. Sliding directly at us was Sisoria, her huge eyes glinting with the light of our orbs.

I knew it was going to be close. "Hurry!" I shouted.

"I am," Shwenn said, racing along just behind me.

It didn't look like the huge snake was going to slow down. Her intention was to crush us under her mighty weight.

Right at the tunnel entrance I jumped toward it. The next moment I felt Sisoria zoom past me and her scaly side clipped my body. I was sent spinning like a top through the air and crashed inside the tunnel.

Dazed, but still in a panic, I looked at the monster's body as it slid past the entrance. Blinking, I looked around. "Shwenn?"

"Here!" She said, picking herself up out a darkened corner she'd been knocked into. "Bruised, but alive."

I staggered to my feet. Behind me I heard the loud sliding noise of Sisoria's belly on the stone floor. She was turning around.

The small tunnel continued into blackness, but thankfully we still had Shwenn's light orbs with us.

"We gotta move, girl!" I said.

I stumbled forward, desperate to get distance between me and the nightmare at my back. The tunnel went straight into the unknown and I ran headlong into it, Shwenn close behind.

After a few paces, a horrific crashing sound behind made me glance back. The great serpent had jammed its head into the entrance, but couldn't get any further. Having seen what it did chasing Witt, I knew it wouldn't be long before she squeezed her way through. I could only pray that whoever built this strange tomb made this tunnel narrower than all the others.

Suddenly, the floor shook, and we pitched to the side, crashing into a wall. Sisoria squeezed her way in further, fracturing the floors and walls in her efforts to get to us.

Full panic gripped at my chest. This thing was going to get us just like it did with Witt.

Recovering from my fall, I pushed myself along the tunnel wall away from the monstrosity behind us. Ahead, I could see a bright chamber or room ahead, glowing red.

Emerging from the tunnel we found ourselves at the edge of a long massive chasm. Below a wide river of lava roiled past. Across the way, directly opposite was another tunnel entrance. It looked as if a bridge had been here before, but had collapsed long ago.

A hissing sound made me turn. The head of Sisoria appeared as she squeezed through the tunnel. Her soulless eyes locked onto us, tongue flickering.

I looked to the other side, again. There was absolutely no way I could jump across, even if my Leap ability had been maxed out.

But thanks to the Cloak of Shadows, I did have one card to play. "Hang onto me!" I said, pulling Shwenn into a hug.

"A bad time for some fun, isn't it?" She said, eyes on the approaching serpent.

"It's always a good time for fun," I said. Focusing on the ledge of the far side I tried to set a Recall point.

As I waited, I could feel Sisoria getting closer and closer. Part of me envisioned getting swallowed alive. Maybe my avatar wouldn't die right away, stuck in the creature's stomach. I shivered, needing to stay focused. All that mattered was the ledge on the other side.

Behind me I heard stone and rock crashing and I knew Sisoria had arrived. She was opening her mouth, but I couldn't look. I heard Shwenn shout a warning.

Recall Point Set.

Bingo!

I used my Teleport ability.

The next instant we stood on the other ledge, the new tunnel entrance before us. A loud angry hiss turned me around.

Back on the other ledge, Sisoria had launched herself out of the tunnel in a bid to swallow us up. But the beast didn't account for the precipitous drop. Her momentum carried her over the edge and she couldn't stop herself from falling. In seconds, the massive creature fell down and splashed into the huge river of molten lava.

I watched in morbid fascination as she thrashed in the liquid rock. Then she sank below the surface and was carried away.

Sighing with relief, I sat down. I could feel that the last few minutes had drenched the inside of my simulation suit with sweat and I waited for it to air out.

"That was incredible!" Shwenn said clapping her hands and laughing. "That was the Cloak, right?"

I nodded. "Pretty handy when it needs to be."

Shwenn looked into the new tunnel. "Shall we go on?"

As if in response to this, the far tunnel suddenly collapsed. The damage Sisoria had done to its structure had been too great.

Stupid game, I thought and stood. The Shadow Blade hadn't been in the chest. I'd lost my opportunity to find it. There was little else for me to do but continue on and hope I found something worthwhile to make up for all my efforts here. And if I managed to get out, maybe I could return in a year's time to look again, but I shuddered at the thought.

Depressed and defeated I turned my back to the molten grave of the serpent god and walked into the tunnel, Shwenn following.

Barely a dozen paces in we came upon a set of stairs descending into darkness. We followed them down, weapons at the ready. It didn't take long to reach a tunnel at the bottom which led into a large square chamber.

At its center sat a block of ivory colored stone. Sticking out of the top of the block, halfway to its hilt, was a sword.

I caught me breath in surprise. Could this be it?

"What?" Shwenn noticing my reaction. "What is it?"

"The sword there, in the stone."

She looked around confused. "I don't see anything. Did you take a hit to the head?"

I was momentarily baffled as to why she couldn't see the sword, then it hit me. It was for Shadows only. Part of its protection was being invisible to all but the class that could use it.

"Trust me, it's there," I said.

Carefully, I walked up to the block, and a message appeared.

Only one with an item of the Shadow Master Set can draw this blade. From the Shadows must come Light!

I felt heady as if about to faint. I couldn't believe it. This was the Shadow Blade, hidden away in a secret tunnel beneath a volcano. Swallowing I gripped the pommel of the sword and pulled.

It came free in my hands and the ivory block shattered into dust to fall into a pile.

You have acquired an item: Shadow Blade (Legendary)
(Shadow Class Only)
(Level 40 required)
(Agility 45 required)
Durability: 60/60
Damage: 200-245
Bonuses:
+40 Damage
+30% Swing speed
+100 Hit Points
+5% Hit Point Regeneration
+1 Swords Skill Level
Shadow Master, Legendary Set Pieces: (2/4)
Cloak of Shadows (set bonus +1 Sneak Skill Level)
Shadow Blade (set bonus +1 Parry Skill Level)
Boots of Shadow (set bonus - unknown)
Shadow Guard (set bonus - unknown)
Full Set bonus - unknown

Finally! I turned the sword around in the light to get a better look at it. The pommel was bound with leather straps with a small curved hook at the base. The blade was long and narrow, its dark metal opaque as smoke.

Sweet! I now had two of the four items of my set. But what now?

Quest complete. 'Obtain the Shadow Blade'

You have found the long lost weapon piece of the Shadow Master. Use it to lead the Light and banish the Darkness.

Shwenn whistled. "Okay, I see it in your hands. Congratulations. Any chance you want to sell it and split the profits?"

"Not in your life!" I said with a laugh.

A small travel gate suddenly appeared in the wall beside us, its silver portal shimmering.

Another message appeared.

Where would you like to be transported?

There was only one place that came to mind.

"Fenwick's Folly," I said. "I'm in need of a good butterscotch ale."

With Shwenn at my side and Shadow Blade in hand, I passed through the gate.

CHAPTER SIXTEEN

We sat in Fenwick's Folly, drinking butterscotch ale and laughing. Having survived the Emerald Caldera, Shwenn was happy to the point of being giddy.

"I swear I'll never take on a quest or go into another instance that has the slightest chance of having a snake in it," she said, downing the last of her ale.

"I can totally identify," I said. "Only another Legendary item could make me tangle with that phobia, again."

The tavern was empty as usual. But Fenwick was content, standing behind the bar and smiling. With two patrons it was like the bar was full to him.

Shwenn said, "I was wondering what happened to Nigel. Is he still cowering in that tunnel?"

"Doubt it," I said. "Either the natives got him or Sisoria did. But it doesn't matter, he's an NPC. Who's to say the instance is even there anymore without us in it?"

"Huh," Shwenn said. "Never thought of it that way. Sort of like that saying if a tree falls in the forest and no one is there to hear, does it still make a sound?"

"If a player isn't present, does the NPC still render?" I said, and we both laughed.

"Another ale, Miss Shwenn?" The barkeep asked.

Shwenn waved her hands. "No, thanks, Fenwick. I'm good for now. Besides, I have to go and start offloading my loot onto the Marketplace. I think this broadsword will be the real money maker of the bunch."

"Good luck!" I said as she went out the door into the streets of Crow's Fall.

"Yourself, Miss Valesh?" Fenwick asked, motioning to my mug.

"Please," I said and turned my attention to the points I'd gotten when I leveled earlier. There hadn't been any time to distribute them before.

Name: Vivian Valesh
Race: Human
Class: Thief
Subclass: Shadow
Level: 47, 1% toward next level
Hit Points: 1300, Mana: 120
Attributes:
Strength: 37
Agility: 46
Constitution: 40
Wisdom: 15
Intelligence: 15
Charisma: 20
You have 2 undistributed Attribute points.

I placed one point into Strength and the other into Agility. The requirements for the Legendary items were high for both, and I didn't want to be caught short if and when I found the next one.

Skills:
Main Skills: (Level 3 or greater)
Archery: Level 8, 82%
Acrobatics: Level 3, 57%
Climbing: Level 7, 22%
Dodge: Level 7, 13%
Parry: Level 6, 59%
Sneak: Level 7, 45%
Swords: Level 9, 74%
Minor Skills: (Under level 3 - Select to view)
You have 5 undistributed Skill points.

I dumped all five points into my Acrobatics, the lowest of my main skills raising it to 70%.

For my three ability points, I put one in Leap, bringing it to 4/10. Then I put the other 2 into Multi-shot raising it to 5/6. This granted me a fifth arrow when used as well as increasing the bonus damage to 20%.

Satisfied, I downed my ale, then slid five gold coins over the bar. "Keep the change," I said, as I stood.

Fenwick beamed. "Please feel free to come back again, Miss Valesh. What will you do now?"

I paused at the door and thought. There were still two other items to complete the Shadow Master set. I could try to find those. But I also had my overall damage output greatly boosted by the Shadow Blade. Maybe I should just go adventuring for a while and test it out. Or I could take on another Shadow for hire job from the forums.

"I don't know, Fenwick," I said. "Let's see what this game throws at me next!" And with that, I pushed my way through the tavern door and out into the streets. Maybe if I couldn't find any trouble on my own, trouble would find me.

As it turned out, I didn't have to wait long at all.

<u>Vivian's adventure continues in</u>
<u>Shadow Gate – Forthcoming</u>

Kingdom Level One
(Kingdom Series Book 1)

A broken kingdom for a reluctant king.

Robert was content with his life as a night-shift janitor. No stress, no worries, and no responsibilities. But this idyllic existence is turned upside down when he suddenly finds himself trapped inside a fantasy Role Playing Game.

Confused and alone he must find a way to escape back to his own world and, more importantly, to his daughter. But to do that he must take up the biggest responsibility of all:

To rule a kingdom.

<u>AVAILABLE NOW</u>

<u>The Big Bag of Infinite Cats</u>
<u>A Supernatural Cozy Mystery</u>

A baffling mystery of ancient magic

When a strange case of a detective being turned to stone stumps local police, retired investigator Mayra Beeweather is asked to assist. One of her tools of the trade is a magical bag which contains an infinite number of cats. Very *special* cats – each with a unique ability to aid in her investigation.

Yet, even with their help, Mayra may not solve the case in time, for she may be the next victim turned to stone.

<u>AVAILABLE NOW</u>

<u>Blackout</u>
<u>A Terrifying Dystopian Thriller</u>

The nightmare begins

In one fell swoop, civilization is changed forever.

No one is unaffected, few are prepared.

Some become survivors, others - easy prey.

Only the strong, and crazy, will survive.

Through the blood and chaos, civilization will be permanently transformed.

And it all begins with one terrifying moment, when the lights go out and never come back on.

Blackout.

<u>AVAILABLE NOW</u>